"When the  ize your mistake in annulment."

The air rushed spun. An annulment? "When are you going to understand that I have no intention of leaving you? Did you not hear me today? I promised to love, honor, and obey you until death parted us."

"I heard your promise. Now obey me and take your things to the next room. I'm tired, and I'd like to go to bed. It's been a long day." He stepped farther into the room and waited.

Numb at this turn of events, Karen gathered her valise and straightened. "David, can't we talk about this?"

"This is not a matter for discussion. Go to bed."

She gathered the lamp and stepped into the hall. He closed the door behind her, shutting her out as effectively as putting out a cat for the night. The final humiliation came when he turned the key in the lock.

ERICA VETSCH is married to Peter and keeps the company books for the family lumber business. A homeschool mom to Heather and James, Erica loves history, romance, and storytelling. Her ideal vacation is taking her family to out-of-the-way history museums and chatting with curators about local history. She has a bachelor's degree from Calvary Bible College in secondary education: social studies. You can find her on the Web at www.onthewritepath.blogspot.com.

Books by Erica Vetsch

HEARTSONG PRESENTS
HP875—The Bartered Bride
HP887—The Marriage Masquerade
HP900—Clara and the Cowboy
HP907—The Engineered Engagement
HP916—Lily and the Lawman
HP928—Maggie and the Maverick

Before the Dawn

Erica Vetsch

Heartsong Presents

For my parents, Jim and Esther Bonam

A note from the Author:
I love to hear from my readers! You may correspond with me by writing:

Erica Vetsch
Author Relations
PO Box 721
Uhrichsville, OH 44683

ISBN 978-1-61626-329-4

BEFORE THE DAWN

one

Karen Worth's mild impatience gave way to moderate annoyance and finally to outright anxiety as she paced the depot. David Mackenzie was never late.

She checked the timepiece hanging on her lapel, comparing it to the solemn face of the Seth Thomas clock on the depot wall beside the ticket window. Her handbag toppled off the valise beside her, and she bent to pick it up. For three quarters of an hour she'd waited here like unclaimed baggage.

Behind his barred cage, the clerk shuffled papers and flicked inquiring glances from under his visor. His pinched mouth twitched, making his mustache stick out like a fussy mouse sniffing a trap.

Where could David be? Karen's visions of a tender, warm reunion with her fiancé evaporated. She crossed her arms and stilled her tapping foot for the tenth time. The unease she'd been trying to ignore over his lack of communication during her absence renewed its assault. The two notes he'd sent the first week of her trip were everything a girl could desire in the way of love letters. Then nothing from him for three weeks.

She'd told herself no end of stories to explain things, but with each passing day, the doubts had grown.

Flap, slap, flap, slap. The clerk worked a rubber stamp as if the papers might somehow escape his inky wrath.

Karen gathered her gloves, her bag, and her courage. She'd simply have to ask him to find her some conveyance after all.

The door crashed open. Whirling, she pressed her hand to her chest then let it drop to her side as she relaxed her tense muscles. Jesse Mackenzie filled the doorway, blocking out the weak sunlight. She offered her hands in greeting, though a tickle of unease scampered through her chest.

The large, gray-haired man strode across the station. "Karen, sorry I'm late." He kissed her offered cheek, brushing her skin with his bushy whiskers.

"Mr. Mackenzie, what a surprise. I expected David."

The older man rubbed his beard and didn't meet her eyes. "Lots going on at the mine and at the house."

The tickle of unease became a tremor. "Where *is* David?"

The clerk cleared his throat, and Jesse glared at him. "We'll sort it out at the house." He whisked up her bags as if they weighed nothing and headed toward the door. She followed in his wake, stopping to tug on her gloves and anchor her hat against the fitful, wind-tossed snowflakes gusting about.

The Mackenzie buggy stood at the hitching rail. Jesse stowed the luggage. Then he helped Karen aboard and let her get settled before spreading the lap robe over her skirts. Cold dampness flowed over Karen when he urged the horses into a brisk trot, and she pulled her cloak tighter. He lifted the reins. "Be time for the bobsled if this snow keeps up."

The horses' hooves made splashing plops in the muddy road of the main thoroughfare. Buggies, wagons, and saddle horses lined the streets. This late in the fall, the trees lifted bare limbs to the sky and the clouds bespoke more snow. Jesse's coat collar stood up around his cheeks, meeting his hat brim at the nape. His gloves creaked on the reins as he slapped them against the horses' rumps.

Karen wrinkled her nose at the familiar tang in the air. Black clouds billowed from the smelter smokestacks night and day. The streets teemed with men of varied nationalities, all drawn to this cleft in the high Rockies by the lure of silver.

When the buggy passed the county registrar's, her heart squeezed a little. She missed the bustle of the office, the desk she had called her own, the neat columns and ledgers. Her boss had relied on her to know where every piece of paper in the office could be located. She had enjoyed the work, but she'd given it up for a very good reason.

Though that reason had failed to meet her train.

Her companion's unusual silence forced the questions out of her. "What's wrong, Jesse? Why didn't David come? Is it something at the mine? Have you found a new ore deposit?" If another rich stope had been located, David, as the mine engineer, would have to be on hand.

Jesse shifted on the seat and urged the horses, though they were already trotting briskly. Bits of slush and dirt flipped backward, spattering the lap robe. "Sure is getting cold out."

Fingers of dread formed a fist in her middle. She clasped her hand over one of his. "Please, just tell me what you're trying so hard not to say."

"I knew I should have sent someone else to pick you up." He scowled as he muttered. "Or brought Matilda along."

Karen gripped his hand tighter. "Please."

"There was an accident—" His shoulders hunched, and he shook the lines again. "Get up there." His words came out in a frosty plume. "At the mine."

Her chest turned frosty, too. An accident. She tried to swallow, but her mouth was slag-heap dry. "Was anyone hurt? Is that where David is? Helping with the rescue and clearing up?"

"The rescuing's been done, and the clearing up, too, mostly."

"Then, what? Jesse, you're scaring me."

He hesitated, dropping his gaze to his hands. "Karen, I hate to be the one to tell you. . . . David was hurt. He's—"

"Is he alive?" Air crowded into the tops of her lungs, and she couldn't draw a deep breath.

"He's alive." Jesse cleared his throat. "But he's blind."

Icy shock gripped the back of her neck. She shook her head, and blackness crept in around the edges of her vision. Gradually the mists in her head cleared. "What happened?"

"There was a cave-in the week after you left for your aunt's. We had just deepened the shaft and started putting in the bracings and square sets when the whole support system gave way. We lost eight men, and another five, including David, were injured. David broke an arm and got hit on the head by a beam. He was senseless for three days. When he came to, he couldn't see a thing. Sam was the one who pulled him from the wreckage. A terrible thing for one brother to have to do for another. Doc says the damage is permanent."

Numbness settled on her, making her lips stiff and her limbs heavy. All the time she nursed her Aunt Hattie in Kansas City, David had been hurt, blinded. Her peeve at his lack of correspondence and his failure to meet her train melted away. What he must've suffered, and she hadn't been there. "We should hurry home, then," she said at last. "He'll be worried if we don't show up soon."

Jesse winced. "Well, Karen, there's one other thing I have to tell you. You see, David isn't expecting you."

"But I sent a telegram with my arrival date and time."

"David hasn't been himself since the cave-in. He dictated a telegram to release you from the engagement." He shook his head, his shoulders bowed, his brow creased in morose lines. "David doesn't want to get married anymore."

The words hit like a physical blow. "I never received a telegram."

Jesse shot her a glance, half-sheepish, half-defiant. "Truth is I didn't send it, though I let him think I had."

"Why not? Why didn't someone tell me what happened?" Heat bloomed in her chest.

"Matilda can explain it all." He shrugged, not looking at her.

"I didn't send the telegram because my son isn't thinking clear. He seems to think—I don't know, that somehow you won't love him anymore now that he's blind. I told him you weren't like that, that he was selling you short, but he won't listen. I figure you showing up might bring him to his senses."

Karen's imagination stirred up scenes in her head of the cave-in, of the dead and dying miners, of her fiancé, broken, wounded, imprisoned in blackness within and without.

Jesse remained silent and frowning until they pulled up in front of the Mackenzie house. Three stories of gleaming windows and gingerbread trim, balconies, turrets, and fish-scale siding rose from the hillside.

Karen leaned forward to glimpse the mansard roof with its widow's walk, the very place David had taken her to propose. They had looked up to the rugged peaks rising all around them and planned out their future together that happy summer evening.

Jesse helped her alight. "You go on in by the fire. Buckford will see to the bags."

She nodded to the faithful houseman who held the door for her. A welcoming blaze crackled in the front parlor fireplace. David's mother, Matilda, rose from her chair and glided across the foyer, as graceful and regal as always. "Karen, my dear." Lamplight raced along her dark-blond hair shot through with silvery strands. "I trust your aunt is on the mend?"

"Aunt Hattie is fine. She sends her regards, and she will see you in two months for the wedding. . . ." Karen's voice trailed off as she looked to Jesse. He shifted from boot to boot and shrugged out of his coat.

"Jesse, you *did* tell her?"

He nodded, his shoulders slumped and his face more lined than Karen remembered.

Matilda gripped Karen's hand. "At first we didn't write because of the ongoing rescue attempts, and then nursing

David. . .and the doctor held out some hope initially that the blindness would be temporary. But as more days went by, we had to resign ourselves to the bitter truth." Matilda sighed. "I am sorry now I didn't write to you immediately. I had hoped to spare you and be able to greet your train with the news that David would fully recover. Can you forgive me?"

Karen nodded. What else was there to do? Nothing could be changed now, and David was foremost on her mind. "Is he upstairs?"

Matilda shook her head. "He's all but barricaded himself in the study, and no matter what we try, he won't come out." The starch and drive Karen always associated with Matilda Mackenzie had been replaced with uncertainty and despair. "We had hoped this anger and lethargy would fade, but he sinks deeper each day. I don't know what to do anymore. I've never prayed so much in my life."

"Maybe I'd better see him first." Jesse tossed his coat at the hall tree. It missed the brass hook and slid to the bench below. "I'll have to fess up to not sending the telegram."

"No, Jesse." Karen stopped him. "I'll go in. I would have come even if you had cabled me David's wishes. Perhaps you're worrying about nothing. Our love is strong enough to survive this." Karen loosened the cape from around her shoulders. She lifted her chin and squared her shoulders, giving Matilda a smile. "I'm sure he'll be glad to see me, especially once I assure him his blindness makes no difference to how I feel about him." She crossed the foyer and eased aside the heavy pocket door to slip inside.

He sat behind the desk in the large red leather chair, his beautiful brown eyes focused on nothing. "Is that you, Buckford?" Dark circles smudged the skin under his eyes, and a greenish blue bruise painted his right temple. Whiskers dusted his cheeks and chin, and his dark-brown hair stood up, as if he'd run his fingers through it many times. He rubbed under the edge of the white sling encasing his arm. "Who's there?"

Karen stirred herself and walked toward him.

He must've heard her skirts rustling, for he asked, "Mother? I don't wish to be disturbed now." He pushed his chair back and braced his good hand on the desk to rise.

Before he could stand, she found her voice. "David?"

He flinched and leaned back in his chair. The skin tightened over his cheekbones, and the bruise stood out as the blood left his face.

"David, it's Karen."

He drew a long breath. "You were told not to come." His flat, emotionless tone chilled her. So far removed from his usual affectionate, charming self, she blinked and searched for a reply. This man before her was a burned-out lamp. Only the charred wick and the smoked glass remained. "Why did you come when I told you not to?"

"David, I. . ." She didn't want to bring his father and the unsent message into this. "I had to come. I had to see you."

"Well, you've seen. You've done your duty, and you can rest your conscience." He rose and faced her.

"My duty? What are you talking about, David?"

"You can go back to your life knowing you made your noble gesture and I refused. I've released you from the engagement, and you won't be tied to a cripple for the rest of your life."

A chill slid down her spine. This wasn't her strong, brave, confident fiancé. This man was broken, his words jagged glass cutting her from his life. She touched his arm.

He jerked away and crashed against the chair, sending it bumping into the wall. She grabbed his wrist to steady him, and he flung her grasp away. "Don't touch me. Don't you understand? Everything has changed now. I don't want you here."

"But, David, I love you." She lifted her chin and straightened her spine. "I can't believe you think I would desert you. Nothing has to change."

"Everything *has* changed. It's over. Just go."

"David, this is far from over. I'll leave you now, but know this: I love you, no matter what has happened to your eyes." Karen fought down the lump in her throat. "I can appreciate the turmoil you must feel right now, but that's no reason to throw away our marriage plans."

He flinched then felt behind him for the chair. He eased down and covered his sightless eyes. "Just go away and leave me alone."

She stood still, not wanting to give up the fight but not knowing what to say or how to get him to change his mind. On the ride from town, she'd been sure that once they were together David's insecurity would vanish. It never once entered her head that he wouldn't change his mind about calling off the wedding.

When she turned to leave the study, her legs seemed to belong to someone else. The hollow ring of her heels on the hardwood floor echoed as if from far away, and her hands were so cold the brass latch on the study door felt warm to the touch.

Jesse and Matilda waited in the foyer. Matilda raised her eyebrows. "What happened?"

Karen shook her head. "He's adamant. The wedding is off." A dozen questions and thoughts clattered in her head, but she couldn't grasp any beyond wondering what she would do now.

Jesse's mouth tightened. "This has gone far enough."

Matilda turned to her husband. "What can we do? I thought things would get better, but they're getting worse and worse. I hoped having Karen here would jolt him out of his misery and remind him that he was still loved, but. . ."

She twisted the handkerchief in her hands.

Jesse scowled. "I think it's time I had a talk with my son." He marched to the door and slid it open.

Karen raised her trembling hand to her temple and closed her eyes. She drew a breath, hoping to shake off the feeling of being caught in a bad dream. But when she opened her eyes, the nightmare remained and her dreams fled.

two

Regret swamped David, pushing against his chest until he found it hard to breathe. It took everything he had not to call out for her, to cling to her and let loose the pent-up grief and fear that had stalked him since the moment he knew he would never see again. He choked back the rock-hard lump in his throat and forced himself to concentrate on holding fast to his decision not to marry Karen.

Heavy footsteps sounded in the hall and then the quick sliding of the door open and shut. Only one man in the house moved like that. David braced himself for parental wrath.

"Well, what do you have to say for yourself?"

Keeping the high back of the office chair between himself and the door, David didn't answer. Karen's perfume lingered in the air, reminding him of all he had lost. She deserved better than half a man, a shell, an object of pity. Any moment now she'd realize he was doing her a favor. And himself. Putting her aside before she had a chance to reject him.

"Well?"

"Leave me alone." David's throat tightened until it ached.

"Not till you face what you've done."

"What I've done?" The chair swiveled toward his father's voice. "You've got nerve coming in here to accuse me. I made my wishes regarding Karen clear."

"You aren't thinking straight right now. You don't mean what you say. We all know you're hurting, but taking it out on those you love isn't going to get your sight back."

"Don't pretend to know how I feel." David got to his feet,

his fists clenched. Impotent humiliation sloshed inside him like kerosene in a can. "It's your fault she's here. You can deal with it." Heat rose up his throat and raced to his hairline at the thought of Karen seeing him like this.

"Why are you acting this way? I raised you better than to be rude to a woman, much less a woman who loves you like Karen does, a woman you promised to marry."

"How can you ask me that? I'm in no condition to take on a wife. What kind of husband would I be? How could I be the leader of my household? Karen might think she still wants to get married, but once she realized I'd forever be dependent on her, she'd regret her decision. Are you forgetting what happened with Uncle Frank and Aunt Bernice?"

Father sucked in a breath as if he'd been gut punched. "I told you never to mention their names in this house again." His words hissed, and David pictured his father's narrowed eyes and clenched teeth. "They're dead. It's finished. Karen would never do something like that to you."

"Circumstances change people."

"What happened fifteen years ago has nothing to do with right now. That's over and done with, and we've all moved on."

"If it's over and done with, why don't you ever talk about it? You want to act like it never happened, which is ridiculous considering Marcus is here as a reminder. You may want to think the situations are different, but I'm not willing to risk it. I'm not dragging this family down that road again."

David followed his father's movements, envisioning his scowling face and restless pacing. Then the movements stopped, and father turned toward him again. "So, what am I supposed to tell Karen?"

The pain in David's head intensified, and his gut twisted. "If you'd have sent the telegram like I told you to, she would've stayed in Kansas City with her aunt." He brushed his fingers against his temple, gauging the soreness that lingered there.

"I'm tired. Please close the door on your way out."

"You can't hide from life forever, David. And I'm not doing your dirty work for you. You and Karen need to sit down and talk about this rationally. She deserves better than you're giving her." Boots clomped on the floor, and the door opened and shut with force.

David massaged his injured wrist in the confining bandages, resigned now to the persistent ache. A wave of panicked remembrance swept over him. The earth trembled, timbers snapped, rocks thundered and cascaded as the mine caved. Thick dust choked him. He coughed and staggered, bracing himself against the unstable walls, dropping his blueprints. A shattered brace hurled downward, landing on his wrist with a sick crunch and bouncing away. All around him men's cries of pain and terror ricocheted off the rock walls. Despite the agony screaming through his arm, he staggered upright, trying to reach the injured. A blinding flash burst through his head when something crashed into his temple and everything went black.

He gulped, trying to force air into his lungs, to remind himself he wasn't trapped in the mine, that he was alive in the study. For the past three weeks, everyone had been telling him he was one of the lucky ones. But the blackness still surrounded him. And it would forever.

There's no reason why that shaft should have collapsed. He bounced his good fist off the desktop. He had gone over the calculations again and again, and each time he concluded the structure should've been stable. As the mine's engineer, it was his duty to see that things proceeded as safely as possible while finding the richest deposits of ore. The deaths and injuries from this disaster rested on his shoulders alone. His father hadn't said so, and neither had anyone else, at least not in his hearing, but he knew the truth. Where had he gone wrong?

All his supports had been kicked right out from under him. Like the mine, his life had caved in, filling his interior with rubble where there had once been a strong support system. Where was his faith? Where was the surety he'd always had that God loved him and heard his prayers? He'd never been so alone and frightened.

God, You've got to help me. You've taken my sight. You've taken my future. The least You can do is help me solve this problem. Show me where I went wrong.

He rose and inched across the room until his hand hit the carved back of the settee. Rounding the rolled arm and claw-and-ball foot, he eased onto the upholstery. A sigh pushed out of his lungs as he slid to his side and put his head on the pillow.

Someone knocked and entered without waiting to be invited.

David stiffened. Did no one in this house know what alone meant?

"It's me, David, Sam."

"What do you want?" David clenched his teeth, in no mood to be berated by his younger brother.

"Just talk." The chair at the end of the settee creaked, and something thunked the low table beside him.

He almost smiled. Mother forbade boots on the table, but she had yet to break either of her sons of the habit. Then he stilled. He would never see his mother's disapproving stare again. "Have you come for your pound of flesh?"

"Nope, I just figured you could explain a couple things for me."

The scent of fresh air and the outdoors filtered toward David off Sam's clothes, something he hadn't smelled in weeks. But then, Sam was free to come and go as he pleased, not imprisoned in darkness in this house. David pictured his brother, as unlike David as could be with his blondish hair and blue eyes, and his easygoing manner and take-life-as-it-comes outlook. Easy enough for Sam to take life as it came. Life had never pummeled Sam as hard as it had David.

"I'll stoke the fire for you. It's almost as cold in here as outside, and that's saying something. The temperature is dropping like an anvil down an air shaft. Snowing, too."

David fumed. He couldn't even do something as simple as lighting the fire. He sat up, scowling. "Leave it."

"Dave, you have to let some of this stuff go. Exploding like a pint of nitro every time someone tries to be nice to you is no way to live." Logs clacked together, paper crumpled, and a match scritched on the hearth. Faint crackles and pops filled the air, along with the smell of burning resin. "There," Sam said, satisfaction in his voice. "Now things'll warm up in here. It'll be more comfortable while we talk."

"There's nothing to talk about."

Sam went on as if he hadn't heard. "I had some time today, while I installed that new pump in shaft two, to do some thinking. I was thinking about that party we had here a couple of months ago."

David gritted his teeth. His insides writhed, and his muscles tensed.

"Engagement parties are always the best kind, don't you think? I tried to get a dance with the prettiest gal at the shindig, but she didn't even notice me. She only had eyes for one fellow that night and saved every dance for him. And that fellow, well, the stars could have fallen from the sky and he wouldn't have known."

"What is your point, Sam?" David tried to ignore the broken glass tearing his heart.

"My point is, that much happiness and caring and loving shouldn't be thrown away. I can see what you're doing, and you think you're doing it for Karen, but you aren't. You're doing it for you. You're too proud for your own good. You want folks to think you're making a noble sacrifice by not tying Karen to a blind man, but the real truth is you are just plain scared. You're scared she won't love you anymore. You're pushing her away before she has a chance to hurt you. You're trying to act like you've stopped loving her." He paused. "Have you? Stopped loving her, I mean?"

Trust Sam to ferret out David's deepest fears and pull them out for casual inspection. "You know I still love her. I've loved her since the moment I first saw her. I will always love her. That's why I have to break the engagement. I love her too much to tie her to a cripple." A giant fist grabbed his heart and squeezed until he couldn't breathe, trapping him as effectively as the cave-in.

"Don't you think Karen should be the one to decide what she wants? I'm not saying it would be easy, and I'm not saying things won't be different than you've planned, but you're not even going to try? I want to know why."

"I won't be the object of her pity. One would think, after all we've been through, that my own family would support me in this decision. I was foolish enough to mention Frank and Bernice to Father, and he still can't bring himself to talk about them. He shut me down."

Sam emitted a low whistle. "That was either brave or stupid, or both. You're lucky he didn't punch you. Anyway, you're not comparing Karen to Bernice, are you? That'd be plain foolish."

David rose on stiff legs. "You're meddling in something that is none of your business. I've made my choice. I'd like you to leave now."

"Running me off won't change anything. You're scared, and you're shoving people aside before they have a chance to reject you or make you feel less of a man." Sam's words hammered like a rock drill, hitting places so raw and fragile it took David's breath away. "You're afraid you're not man enough to marry Karen and let her love you." The chair creaked, and Sam's voice came from higher up. "Don't throw away everything you have with Karen. She still loves you. She can help you through this. We'd all like to help."

"I don't want to *need* your help. Can't you understand that?" David flung wide his arm, lost his balance, and toppled. He crashed into a marble-topped table, hit the glass lamp standing on it, and sent it to the floor. The smell of kerosene enveloped him just before his head hit the rug, exploding bright, white stars in his brain.

"David?" Sam's hands reached for him. "Are you all right?"

David shoved aside his brother's help. Sharp pain stabbed up his broken arm. Gasping for breath, he held his good hand to his head. "Just leave me alone. Why don't you just get out of here?"

❧

Karen jumped when the lamp broke, covering her mouth and gripping the edge of the study door.

Sam motioned her to be quiet. "At least let me help you get up. You don't want to cut yourself on this glass."

When David stood upright, cradling his injured arm to his middle, Karen exhaled and bit her lip.

Sam brushed at David's clothes, until David shoved his hand away. "Go away, Sam."

Karen jumped when someone touched her arm. Buckford stood at her elbow. She drew him away from the door to whisper, "A lamp got broken."

"I'll see to it."

Sam edged through the doorway, glanced at Buckford's retreating back, and then met Karen's eyes. Everything she'd overheard watered her parched heart. Tears blurred her vision, and pain, sweet and sharp, flowed through her chest.

David still loved her.

She swung from hope to despair. What good did his still loving her do if he remained adamant about not marrying her? And who were Frank and Bernice, and why hadn't she heard of them before?

All through dinner—at which David did not make an appearance—she played the what-if game. What if Aunt Hattie hadn't gotten ill? What if Karen had been here when the accident occurred? Would it have made any difference? What if David didn't change his mind? What would she do? Without David, Aunt Hattie was the only family she had left. Her thoughts scampered like squirrels in an oak tree while everyone transferred to the parlor.

Sam dropped onto the settee and plonked his boots onto the table. At his mother's frown, he eased his feet back, a sheepish grin twisting his mouth.

Jesse took up his post by the mantel, hands behind his back, staring into the flames.

Buckford carried in a silver tray of coffee cups and poured the fragrant drink.

"Did you get the lamp cleaned up?" Sam took a cup. "I'm sorry about the mess. I got Dave riled up."

The houseman nodded. "Everything is tidy now. He's resting, though he didn't eat much of the meal I took to him." Buckford's brows descended and he shook his graying head.

Matilda cleared her throat and smoothed her skirts. "We've accommodated David, hoping the bitterness would pass, and now that we can see it's lingering, we haven't changed our ways."

"What do you plan to do?" Karen pressed her lips together to stop their trembling.

Matilda's chin came up. For the first time that day, Karen felt like smiling. The fighting glint had returned to the older woman's eyes. If anyone could right this ship, it was Matilda Mackenzie. "The first thing we have to do is stop showing pity. Feel sorry for him, cry for him if you must, but never in his presence. David must learn to live with his blindness, and so must we. We'll find ways to help him be more independent, and we won't take no for an answer."

At her words, Jesse came to stand behind her, his hands blanketing her shoulders and squeezing.

She looked up at him, the affection between them evident even after all their years of marriage. "This will be difficult and, knowing David, will take more than enough patience from all of us, but I refuse to let him shut himself away from the rest of the world forever."

Karen cradled her coffee, trying to warm her fingers. Sleet pinged against the windowpanes, and the wind whistled under the eaves. "Do you think he'll change his mind about the wedding?"

No one spoke for a moment. Then Matilda leaned forward. "Karen, you must make very sure that David is still what you want. You do realize the blindness won't go away? You can't marry him and then decide in a few months or even years that you don't want all that goes along with being married to a blind man."

Jesse frowned and harrumphed.

Matilda tucked her lower lip in for a moment, her eyes tensing. "Well, she has to be sure."

Karen glanced from Jesse to Matilda, then at Sam, who put his cup down and contemplated the crown molding. A strange undercurrent flowed through the room and around Karen. She frowned and set her cup down to clench her hands in her lap. "I'm sure. I love David, and I know he loves me." Her glance flicked back to Sam whose mouth quirked. He nodded encouragement to Karen. "David, blind or not, is what I want, and I'm willing to fight for him. I'm willing to do whatever I can to assure him of my love."

Matilda leaned forward and patted Karen's arm. "Good. Then the changes for David will begin in the morning. It will take all of us together to bring this about. He's gotten a fair dose of stubbornness from each of his parents. If you are certain, then I think I have a plan that will at least wake him out of his malaise." She glanced over her shoulder at her husband. "Jesse and I have discussed this, and we're in complete agreement." Jesse returned his hand to her shoulder. "Sam, you will need to ride to town early with a message for Josiah Fuller." She outlined the bare bones, and Karen could hardly believe what she'd come up with.

When she finished, Sam picked up one of the chess pieces from the table beside him and tossed it lightly into the air. "This could prove to be mighty interesting. Dave won't know what hit him. I hope you know what you're doing."

Matilda sighed and closed her eyes, leaning her head to the side to rest on Jesse's arm. "I have no confidence that I know what I'm doing, but we can't keep on as we are."

After chasing ideas and posing possible scenarios for another hour, Jesse finally sent everyone to bed.

Karen went through her nightly ablutions, her head and heart heavy, but once under the coverlet, sleep eluded her. Everything they'd talked about tumbled around in her head, and she sifted through what David's blindness would mean to her.

She searched her soul long and hard. Though she had given Matilda her assurance that David's condition made no difference in her love for him, she examined her heart to make absolutely certain. Could she spend her life happily married to a blind man? Would he give her the chance?

Flipping back the covers, she prowled the confines of her room, crossing and re-crossing the moonlit carpet, praying, wrestling, arguing, and praying some more. The limitless questions came from every corner of her mind, until at last she hit on the one question that answered the rest. It wasn't a matter of would she be able to live happily with David, but rather would she be able to live happily anywhere without him.

three

In his dreams David could still see. Colors so vibrant and motion so vivid and beautiful it almost hurt. Sunshine bathed every flower and mountain peak in golden light. Every leaf and blade of grass stood out in crisp, glorious detail. He felt strong and steady, grounded and yet ready to soar like a bird. Karen stood before him in a flowing golden gown. She held an armful of pink roses, and her face glowed with love. She held out her hand to him, beckoning him to take it and walk with her along a creek bank where diamonds of light shattered off the water. His fingers touched hers, and warm, white brightness surrounded them.

Then he opened his eyes.

Dreams and sight vanished, swallowed by perpetual dark. Reality sat on his chest like a grinning stone gargoyle.

He ignored the door opening and the light footsteps tapping on the study floor, burrowing his head into the pillow and resigning himself to another dark day. His ankle knocked the end of the settee. He probably should sleep in his own bed instead of this narrow sofa, but that would mean navigating the house, and he preferred the safety and familiarity of the study.

"David, get up. It is after ten." His mother's voice cracked like a twig breaking.

He groaned and flexed the fingers of his mending arm.

She prodded his bare shoulder. "Get dressed. You have ten minutes. Your presence is required in the parlor. A family meeting."

David grimaced at her brisk tone. "Have it without me.

You don't need me there."

"Nonsense. You're the guest of honor. I suppose, if you force us, we could hold the meeting in here with you in your current state of dishevelment." She marched across the room and closed the door before he could muster another protest.

Stung, David moaned and tried to untangle his legs from the blanket. The clock ticked as he cradled his forehead in his good hand. He had no doubt Mother would make good her threat to hold a family meeting here with him in his nightwear should he fail to appear in the parlor.

He groped for his clothing, his head pounding so hard he could almost hear it. Biting down the bile rising in his throat, he castigated himself for being too proud to ask for assistance in taking his pain medications the night before. Though he would have welcomed the relief from the headache, he couldn't bring himself to ask for help after throwing everyone out of the study. His conscience pricked at behaving so poorly, but he quashed it.

David managed to dress, and after a fumbling search, found his boots. Unshaven and in yesterday's clothes, he must look like a saddle tramp. Served them right for rousting him out when he felt so poorly. If the family wanted a meeting, they'd take him like this or not at all. He dragged across the study and groped for the door.

Their voices traveled across the foyer from the parlor—his father's loud, Sam's softer but just as insistent. Sam started again, but Mother interrupted him.

He couldn't hear Karen. She must've gone, then. Her absence made him ache, but a small part of him felt vindicated. She'd left him. That proved he'd done the right thing.

He inched his way to the parlor doorway, noting that all the voices had stopped. They were watching him. Keeping an arm straight out in front of him, he groped for the doorjamb. Fabric swished, telling him his mother's location at the same time his hand hit the fringe decorating the doorway. A boot scuffed and coins jingled in a pocket. Father, by the fireplace.

"Good morning, David." Mother's voice was as bland as cream. "Please, sit down." She must be in her favorite chair near the hearth. "There is an empty chair just a few steps in front of you." Her voice reminded him of a crisp winter morning. He grasped the back of the chair and directed himself into it, determined to hear what they had to say then retreat back to the study.

Father said nothing, but the poker clattered against the grate. The mine collapse, their argument of yesterday, his refusal to marry Karen—these things stood between him and his father, and the gap appeared to be widening.

"Morning, Dave." Sam, off to the left by the bay window.

His mother cleared her throat. "We have much to discuss, and I don't want to get sidetracked. David, I feel that we owe you an apology."

He lifted his head and raised his brows.

She continued. "We've done you a grave disservice. As a family, we have coddled you, catered to you, and cloistered you. That was an error on our part. We've allowed you to become so self-centered as to be harmful to yourself. For that I apologize, and believe me, we will rectify this situation."

He gripped the arms of the chair, and his back straightened. Every muscle in his face tensed as he bit back a hot protest. If they'd dragged him in here just to chastise him, then he was leaving. He braced his hands on the arms of the chair to rise.

"Sit still. I'm not finished." His mother's dagger-like tone froze him. "No longer will you shut yourself away in the study like a coward. I have always enjoyed that room and see no reason why I should be deprived of its use so you can flee from your problems. You will sleep in your bedroom from now on. You will also eat your meals with us in the dining room. I know it makes you uncomfortable, but if you can't feel safe learning and making mistakes here with the people who love you, you'll never go out that front door again."

David flinched at her tone. He had no desire to go out the front door. He only desired to be left alone. Cotton dryness spread through his mouth, and his arm ached anew.

Mother continued, and his stomach clenched. "You will learn to dress yourself properly, to care for your personal hygiene, and to be responsible for yourself. You will learn to face your life as it is now and show some courage. We will procure whatever outside help we need to assist you. Rest assured, we will not leave you alone in this."

The words David forced out through tight lips tasted like ashes. "You ask too much."

"You are still a very valued member of this family, and the problem has been we've not asked enough of you," Mother shot back, her words peppering him like buckshot. "We are all agreed on this. Buckford will spend the morning cleaning the study so we may have use of it again. You will stay here and keep Karen company for the time being. Her guest should arrive before too long."

His face heated, and his teeth ground together. Karen was here? And she'd heard every word of his humiliation at the hands of his family. He swallowed hard and fumed at the high-handed way his family insisted upon running his life. Further proof of his helplessness.

His father and brother stalked out, their footsteps receding and the front door slamming. Mother pressed her hand on his shoulder as she passed. He refused to acknowledge her, and with a sigh, her touch dropped away. Her light footsteps crossed the parlor and receded. Then he was alone with Karen.

"I thought you'd left," he said, keeping his voice expressionless.

"Your mother invited me to stay as her guest. I accepted."

Her voice cut through him.

He closed his eyes against a wave of love for her, but he forced himself to harden his heart against it. Though he longed for the comfort and assurance of her arms, to hear her say once again that his blindness didn't matter, he refused to give in to the need. Whatever declarations she might make now would only make her leaving that much more difficult. "You're expecting a guest? It seems a bit soon to be entertaining, having just broken off our engagement."

She was quiet for a moment then spoke slowly, as if measuring her words. "If you will recall, I am not responsible for our broken engagement." Her voice turned away from him.

His nails indented his palms. How he wished he could see her, to look into her eyes once more, to ascertain if she was hurting or if she was relieved the wedding had been cancelled.

A teacup rattled in a saucer. "David, I wish you'd reconsider your decision."

"No. There will be no reconsidering. Who are you expecting?" He could've bitten his tongue for asking.

"Actually, I had need of a lawyer. Sam took a message to town early this morning and brought back word that Mr. Fuller would see me today."

"A lawyer? What for?"

"I don't think it would be prudent to discuss this subject with you before speaking to my lawyer."

The knocker banged on the front door. Deliberate, slow footsteps—Buckford's—crossed the foyer. The door swung open.

"I have an appointment with Miss Worth, Buckford. Something about filing a lawsuit?" Fuller's voice boomed, as big and rotund as he.

"This way, sir."

A gust of chilly air swirled into the room.

"Hello, David. Ah, Karen, my dear."

David staggered to his feet. "What's this about a lawsuit?" He turned back toward Karen. "Who's getting sued?"

"Why, *you*, David. I'm suing you for breach of promise for breaking our engagement." Her voice hitched, then steadied. "If you will excuse me, I have things to discuss with my lawyer in private." Her gardenia perfume wafted toward him, contrasted by the steel in her voice.

David stood rooted to the spot as their footsteps faded down the hall. Suing him? Breach of promise? The hammer and anvil in his head pounded out a beat in time with his heart, and weakness crept over him. He groped behind himself to find the chair once more and sank into it.

She wasn't serious, was she?

four

Karen bit her lip and led Mr. Fuller to the dining room. David's vulnerability made her want to give in, to assure him she didn't mean it, that it was all a hoax. He must've felt as if everyone had turned their backs on him, but what else could she do? David's parents thought it would shake him up, and they knew him well. She would go along with it for a while, and they had assured her she could back down any time.

Karen seated herself at the dining room table and poured Mr. Fuller a cup of coffee. She'd always liked him from her days as a clerk in the land office. Those halcyon days when she had been new in town and on the cusp of falling in love with the handsomest man she'd ever met.

"A terrible thing." The lawyer bent his round frame and hung over the chair for a moment before he dropped onto the needlepoint seat covering with a sigh. "I wish there was something I could do for him." He opened his case, took out a thick law book, paper and pencil, and tapped the pages into a neat pile. His fussing continued until the papers and the pencil were perfectly aligned and squared up before him. "Let me make sure I have this clear." He rubbed his side-whiskers and consulted her note. "David has called off the engagement and you'd like to sue him for breach of promise?"

"Actually, I don't really want to sue him. I just want to get him to change his mind, but I have to look like I am suing him."

"This isn't a joke, right?" He regarded her soberly, his small eyes boring into hers. For all his jocularity and bonhomie, Josiah Fuller had a reputation as a shrewd lawyer. "From the moment I file the lawsuit, it will become public record. David

30

will be served with papers and the waiting period will begin. He will have thirty days to reach a settlement out of court or the case will go on the docket to be heard."

"If he hasn't changed his mind within thirty days, I will have failed anyway. I'll withdraw the lawsuit."

"So you don't intend to take this to court?"

"No. I just want him to think I will. I'm trying to snap him out of this malaise and get him to realize we belong together. I love him too much to walk away from him, especially now." She ran the tip of her finger over her lower lip. "Mrs. Mackenzie said if I love David then I should fight for him and let nothing, not even David, deter me. I intend to do just that."

Warmth flooded Mr. Fuller's eyes, and his cheeks jiggled as he laughed. "I don't think David knows what a gem he has in you, Karen." His whiskers twitched as he cleared his throat and squared up the already square papers before him. He poised the pencil over the pages. "I haven't handled a breach-of-promise suit before, so I bent the ear of a colleague of mine who has experience in these matters." He paused to write a line in precise all-uppercase letters, then withdrew another sheaf of papers from his bag. "This is a copy of his latest breach-of-promise lawsuit, which should give us a framework to pattern our document after. Let's go through this step by step and see what we have."

For the next hour, Karen answered his questions. He consulted his casebook and papers frequently, pausing to think between questions, probing methodically through her courtship and engagement, filling out page after page with her answers.

At last he sat back and laced his fingers over his vest. "My dear, you have the most compelling case I've heard. Much better than any in here." He nodded toward the casebook. "If David doesn't change his mind, you would be sure to win in court. Perhaps you can explain to me why you wouldn't go through with the lawsuit when you're sure of winning?"

"It's wrong for one Christian to take another to court."

"It's wrong for a young man to promise to marry a girl and then yank all that away, leaving her with nothing." Fuller closed the papers into a file folder and shut the book. "As for one Christian suing another. . .if they didn't, I would be out of business. You'd be surprised at how many 'Christians' I have for clients."

"Just because a behavior is prevalent doesn't make it right." One of Aunt Hattie's maxims came out before Karen knew it. What would she tell her aunt about the wedding? A sigh forced itself past the lump in her throat.

"He's done you a grievous wrong, and you deserve something besides his broken promises. The court will take into account his accident and his blindness, but they'll also take into account that he's a member of one of the wealthiest families in Colorado. He promised you that you would be a part of that family, and now he's withdrawn that promise. No one would blame you for suing."

Karen shook her head. "That wouldn't be right. This isn't about the money. It never has been. I'd marry David if he didn't have a penny. The lawsuit is just to jar him, to make him realize he's hurting other people—besides himself—with his actions."

Josiah stood and patted her shoulder. "I'll be back this afternoon with the papers. Until then, it would probably be best if you didn't discuss anything with David."

"I don't think that will be a problem."

&.

David stayed in the parlor until he heard Fuller leave.

Suing him. He never would've believed it of his gentle Karen. It just proved he was right to call off the wedding. If she could turn on him so quickly, how long would it have taken her to despise him after they said their vows?

Sinking lower into the chair, he tried to block out Mother's voice demanding he show some courage, face his life, and stop moping for how it used to be. He'd never considered himself a particularly brave man, but neither did he consider himself a coward. Until now. He'd add it to his list of shortcomings.

He pushed himself upright and probed his way out to the staircase. Holding the banister, he kicked his toe out to measure the steps. Why hadn't he ever counted them before?

Turning to the left at the top, he brushed the wall, inching forward. His parents' door first, then the guestroom Karen used, Sam's door, turn to the right at the end of the hall, straight ahead five steps, his own bedroom door. Relief that he'd made it this far alone trickled through him.

He opened the door and stepped in. Freshness, as if the window had been left open recently, greeted him. The bed sat before him and a little to the left. His hand glided over the smooth comforter. Though no longer able to see the rich dark blue, it surprised him that he could enjoy the texture of the fabric so much. His hand wrapped around the newel post at the foot of the bed, feeling the ridges of the carved walnut, smelling the lemony, beeswax aroma of the polish Sally Ann used.

The light scent made him aware of his own smell. With a wry twist of his lips he turned to find the dresser. With tentative fingers, he searched the drawers, feeling the fabrics, trying to identify what shirt he held. At last his fingers brushed pin-tucked linen. His favorite white shirt. Laying it across the foot of the bed, he turned to select a pair of pants and some socks. Blue, brown, black? He slammed the drawer shut.

Removing his rumpled shirt, he groped his way to the washstand. To his surprise he found the water in the pitcher warmed. Buckford must have known about the family meeting and put his money on Mother to have her way. A wry smile twisted his lips once again.

Through all his ablutions, his mind mulled the pending lawsuit. He'd underestimated Karen's resolve. But, then again, she had underestimated his.

He managed to cut himself at least twice, but he did get shaved and dressed. Now for some coffee and pain medicine.

He made it to the bottom of the stairs again without mishap. His legs shook, reminding him of all the time he'd spent bedridden over the past month. A yeasty, warm fragrance came from the back of the house, drawing him down the hall to the kitchen. He pressed his hand against the swinging door and eased it aside.

"Mr. Mackenzie."

"Mrs. Morgan." David acknowledged the woman who had cooked for the family for several years. "Could I have some coffee, please?" He concentrated so hard on remembering the layout of the kitchen that he made it halfway across the room before he realized he had closed his eyes. A rueful chuckle rose to his throat. He found a chair and sat down at the table.

"I must say, sir, you are looking much better. You've taken your sling off. Is your arm healing, then?" She set the coffee down in front of him.

"It's fine." He groped for the cup. "You wouldn't happen to have the laudanum, would you? For my headache?"

"I do, and I'll add it to your coffee directly. I've been baking today. Would you like a muffin or some fresh bread?" Cupboards opened and cutlery clanked.

"No, thank you, Mrs. Morgan, just the coffee. Has Mother been in to talk to the staff?"

She hesitated. "Yes. She came in and had a few words with Buckford and myself and Sally Ann."

"And what did my formidable mother say?"

"Well, now. . ."

"It's all right, Mrs. Morgan. Just tell it straight."

He pictured the comfortably upholstered Mrs. Morgan crossing her short arms under her considerable bosom and tilting her head before speaking. "She said no more trays in the study and no more coddling. She said you wouldn't learn to live in this house without your sight unless we made you, and no matter how hard it seemed, or how you might fight us, we weren't to give in."

He pursed his lips. "No quarter given, eh?"

"That's right, sir. Buckford said we had to be obeying the missus, and he told Sally Ann he'd take care of your room from now on himself. Here's your coffee. You sure you won't have a bite to eat?"

"No, thank you. I couldn't eat a thing right now. Maybe later."

She harrumphed.

He couldn't seem to please anyone in this house today.

⁂

"The lawyer has returned, and David is waiting with him in the dining room." Buckford's eyes held a note of laughter. Not much escaped his knowledge in the Mackenzie abode. Karen had no doubt he was fully aware of the pending lawsuit.

She nodded and braced her shoulders for the coming battle. Her resolve must not waver.

"Gentlemen." She lifted her eyebrows in a silent question to her lawyer as she entered.

Both men rose and David cleared his throat. "Karen, we need to talk." He had shaved and dressed in clean clothes, as if preparing to do battle. At least she'd gotten him to do that much.

"Of course."

Mr. Fuller held a chair for her and then seated himself at the end of the table.

Karen smoothed her skirts and forced her hands to relax in

her lap. "Please, sit down, David."

Tiredness etched his pale face. The lingering signs of pain and illness clung to him, but he held himself erect, as if he had no intention of giving in to weakness.

Forcing himself to be strong all alone broke her heart while at the same time brought out her fighting side. He had made the choice to separate himself, pushing everyone away. And why?

David released a slow breath. "I'm sure you'll agree it would be in everyone's best interest to reach a settlement outside the courts."

Karen kept her voice even. "It would be in everyone's best interest if the wedding went ahead as planned."

"No."

Fuller smoothed his whiskers and laced his fingers together, bracing his weight on his forearms. "We would be interested in hearing your proposed settlement, but rest assured, David, we will not be easily satisfied. You've done grievous harm to my client, and we are seeking due compensation."

"Your client? Use her name, Josiah. We're all friends here. Or at least we used to be." A whisper of regret clung to his words. He pressed his lips together and placed his hands flat on the table. "I am a fair man. I realize Karen's life has been disrupted by all of this. I'm not averse to compensating her for her troubles."

Compensate her for her troubles? He made her sound like one of his employees. "Just how much would you deem suitable?" Karen leaned forward, ignoring the damping motions from her lawyer. "I don't want your money, David. I want your heart." She twisted the garnet on her finger, the ring she hadn't removed since the night he placed it there. "You said I would always have your heart, but you've taken it back and pushed me aside. I put my future in your hands, and you've dropped it like an old teacup. I'm trying to pick up the broken pieces. I've got no job, no home, and no future." She rose and put both palms on the table, leaning forward. "Open the door on that self-imposed prison of pride you're locked in and think of someone besides yourself for a moment."

David flinched but rallied. "And whom are *you* thinking of in this lawsuit? Yourself, right?"

"Would you believe me, David, if I said I was thinking of you?" She straightened. "Of course you wouldn't. You've wrapped yourself so deep in your hurt there's no room for anything or anyone else. You act as if our love meant nothing to you."

He sucked in a breath, and for a moment she thought she had gone too far. How had they so quickly descended into name-calling and accusations? "I'm sorry, David. I apologize for my bad manners. Mr. Fuller, if you could leave the papers you've drawn up, I'll go over them and get them back to you."

"Of course, my dear. Why don't you show me out?" He gathered himself and heaved to his feet. "David, I am sorry about all of this, but Karen is my client, and I must do my best to guard her interests."

She walked Fuller to the door and took the papers he offered her.

"Read them carefully, and if they meet with your approval, sign them and return them to me. And think about what I said. You have a very strong case."

When he'd gone, she leaned against the door and swiped at the tears on her cheeks. Was this doing any good at all? She and David were further apart than ever.

☙

Buckford entered the dining room, his soft tread as recognizable to David as his lined face. "Mr. Quint is here to see you."

"Marcus?" David's cousin hadn't visited once since the

cave-in. Not that David really blamed him. No doubt he'd been busy with the clean-up at the mine and running the office in David's absence. Sick calls probably weren't high on his to-do list. "Is he in the parlor?"

"Yes, sir."

"I know Mother instructed you not to lead me around, Buckford, but for the sake of greeting my guest in a timely manner and without benefit of a black eye from walking into a door, could you escort me?" He gripped Buckford's arm, grateful for the support.

Gathering his courage and his wits—both scattered from his encounter with Karen and Fuller—he greeted his cousin. "It's good of you to come, Marcus."

Buckford placed David's hand on the back of a chair.

Hoping Marcus wouldn't comment on how he inched around, David eased onto the seat.

"David, I feel terrible I haven't been to visit you before now. Things have just been so busy."

David formed Marcus's image in his mind, tall and slender, sandy brown hair just beginning to thin. A capable assistant.

"Have you made much progress? Are things getting back to normal?" It hurt to even ask. Not only had David caused the deaths and injuries of several good men, he had crippled himself to the point where he was helpless to make any sort of amends. He couldn't even assist with righting the damage at the mine and getting production under way once more.

Marcus sighed, and David could only imagine the horror of pulling the broken bodies of friends and co-workers out of the depths of the mine. "All the bodies have been recovered. The shaft is a shambles, though. It has taken all this time just to clear it out."

"What are the workers saying?"

"Accidents are a part of mining, David. You can't blame yourself. Sometimes things happen that we don't intend. You can't plan for every contingency."

The sadness in Marcus's voice prodded all the sore places in David's heart. "How could I have miscalculated so much? The square sets were in place and should have been more than adequate for the load. I can't think of a single reason why that part of the shaft should have collapsed. Be honest with me, Marcus. I know I can trust you. Tell me, what did I do wrong?"

"You can't beat yourself up over this. Things happen and sometimes we never know the cause. You can't know how sorry I am about your. . .injury. That's what I really wanted to say. I didn't come to talk about the mine. I came to say how sorry I am that all this happened, and now I hear your marriage is off, too."

"You heard? How?"

"Sam told me. Is she really suing you?"

"Word gets around quick. Yes, the engagement is off, and yes, Karen is suing me. It seems God is not on my side at the moment. Nothing but lightning bolts from the blue."

"Was Karen horrified that you are. . . ?"

"You can say the word, Marcus. I'm blind." David gritted his teeth. When would people stop dancing around the fact? He didn't want people to talk about his blindness, but neither did he want them to skirt around the fact. "Karen seems to think my circumstances should have no bearing upon our wedding plans, but that's naive. I broke the engagement for her." Though he'd had no idea she would resort to legal action. "I'm trying to spare us both a lot of heartache. If anyone could understand my motives, it's you."

Marcus shifted. "You're right. Nobody would understand like me." He leaned forward and gripped David's shoulder. "It would take a brave man to face the fact that things won't be the same from now on. Releasing Karen is the only logical thing to do."

"I wish other people would realize that it's for the best." David clenched his fists, forcing himself to believe his own words. "I have a favor to ask of you."

"Anything. You know that."

"Help me. Help me find out why the mine collapsed. Help me keep it from happening again. I need you to be my eyes at the mine. I need you to go over those blueprints, the load figures, rock samples. . .everything."

"Are you sure you should be worrying about that sort of thing now? You need to heal. It hasn't been all that long since the accident. Give yourself some time. You have this situation with Karen to deal with. I can handle things at the mine."

"I know you can. It's just. . .I need to know what happened."

"I'll do what I can, but I doubt we will ever know what really happened."

"Thank you, Marcus. I knew I could count on you."

five

Karen waited on David's next move. He followed the letter of the new law of the house, showing up for dinner and spending the evenings with the family in the parlor or study, but the spirit of the law he ignored completely, picking at his food and sitting in stony silence.

Three tense days passed in which she got little sleep and prayed for a breakthrough. On the evening of that third day, she joined the Mackenzies in the parlor.

Sam and Jesse began a game of chess while Matilda dug yarn from her workbasket. Her brows lowered as her knitting needles clicked.

Karen couldn't take her eyes from David who sat by the fireplace, his profile outlined by the reflection of the flames. He held a pencil between his palms, rolling it back and forth, his sightless brown eyes focused on nothing.

If only he would let her past the wall he'd erected between them. She longed to soothe his hurt, to hold him and have him hold her. Why couldn't he realize she needed him, not for his eyes but for his strength of spirit, his integrity, the caring heart she knew still lived somewhere inside him? Why couldn't he realize the more-than-awkward position he'd put her in by breaking the engagement? She picked up her book, and though she turned the pages, she comprehended nothing of the story. When Matilda sighed and frowned at the yarn in her hands, Karen lowered her book and asked, "Is that a difficult pattern?"

"No, it's just that my state of mind is evident in whatever I'm knitting. If I'm tense, the stitches get tighter. These last

two rows are so tight the yarn is squeaking on the needles."
She thrust the points into the ball and stuffed the entire
project back into her workbasket. "Let's talk of something
else."

Sam looked up from his game. "How's the arm feeling,
David? You've quit wearing the sling."

"It's fine."

Matilda lowered her chin and folded her hands in her lap.
"Karen, I understand you met with Josiah Fuller again today.
How did that go?"

David's head snapped around to face their voices.

Matilda had dropped the cat among the pigeons, and her
pale blue eyes gleamed with satisfaction.

"As well as could be expected." Karen unfolded the
document Matilda had requested she bring along after
supper. "He brought me my own copy of the lawsuit. Would
you like to read it?"

"It might be best if you read it out loud, since it concerns
all of us." The older woman's voice was as bland as rice
pudding, but she had David in her sights.

David scowled, and Karen's hands trembled as she smoothed
the papers on her lap. Her heart thrummed in her ears. So
much hinged on David's reaction. Her voice shook a bit as she
read through the opening paragraphs but steadied as she got to
the heart of the matter.

"*. . .did freely and publicly announce their betrothal and
intention of joining together in marriage. Such being the case,
the private setting aside of the betrothal will substantially
damage the plaintiff's ability to obtain a suitable marriage in
the future, as well as severely affect her good reputation. The
circumstances of the breach of promise defame the plaintiff's good
name and standing in the community. The plaintiff cites the
economic hardship that has befallen her as a result of the breach of*

promise on the part of the defendant. She gave up her employment situation at the urging of her betrothed, and the position has been filled by another."

Jesse grinned like a well-fed cat, his arms banded across his broad chest, his booted ankles crossed toward the hearth. Sam tipped a pawn on edge and rolled it in a circle, not looking up, though an arrow of concern formed between his brows.

When Karen got to the monetary compensation clause, the pencil David had been toying with snapped. "That's outrageous." The words burst from him like bullets from a gun. "That sum is preposterous. This entire situation is preposterous."

Karen lowered the papers, not trusting herself to speak. She wanted to tell him this was a farce, that she had no intention of going through with it, that she loved him and wanted him to *want* to be married to her.

Matilda nodded, a smile playing around her lips. She must think her plans were working at least in part. David was talking to them.

"Whew, Karen, that's a sight of money." Jesse whistled. "Fuller thinks he can get you that much?"

David shot to his feet, sending his chair crashing into the wall. "Over my dead body. And, Father, I can't believe you aren't livid about—"

Matilda cut him off. "There is a simple solution to this problem, David. I believe Karen is entitled to something out of this whole affair. If you aren't prepared to do the right thing by her, then she deserves compensation. Of course, you could end this entire business by marrying her. The family is agreed in this, and it is what you want, isn't it, Karen?"

"With all my heart," Karen whispered, choking back the tears.

David snorted. "That is not going to happen. Karen, you've lost your senses. You will not coerce me this way. Neither will you rob my family in this manner. Mother, I've abided by your new rules, but as of now, my evening is finished. Good night."

David skirted the settee and ran straight into the potted palm on the table by the door. The pot teetered for a moment, then crashed to the floor, shattering and sending dirt and palm fronds across the rug. Redness barged up David's neck and across his high cheekbones. He stumbled through the wreckage and groped for the door handle before anyone could move.

Karen's mouth hung open. She was the one who had lost her senses? She rose to go after him.

Matilda tried to restrain her. "No, Karen, don't back down now."

"Don't worry." She gently removed Matilda's hand from her arm. "I have no intention of backing down." Her footsteps rang on the foyer floor. "David Mackenzie, stop this instant."

He stopped, his hand gripping the rail, halfway up the staircase.

She lifted her hem and marched up the steps. "How dare you! How dare you claim I am out of my mind or somehow out of order in seeking recompense. I didn't break this engagement. You did. You called the tune, now you can pay the piper. You've been nothing but rude and cold since I returned, and your treatment of your mother was atrocious. You owe her an apology for your unkind words, and you broke her vase and didn't even have the decency to say you were sorry."

"My mother's vase?" His head tilted and his eyebrows rose. Then his face hardened once more. "When you receive your payout from the lawsuit, you can buy her a new one."

His voice flicked at her, and she burned to grab his shoulders and shake some sense into him, to make him realize how much he was hurting all of them, how much he was hurting himself. "Stop being so difficult. I don't want the money. I only want to marry you. I love you, David, and I know you love me. Why must you be so blind?"

He froze, his face going white at her words.

She wanted to call them back, but it was too late.

A ripple went through his body, as if she had struck him.

Her apology was halfway up her throat when she touched his arm.

But he stiffened and thrust her hand aside. "*My dear. . .*"

She winced at the endearment he used to say with such tenderness.

"You claim you still want to marry me? You say you'll sue me if I don't capitulate? Well, if nothing else will please you, and since you have the support of my entire family, then I will marry you and leave you to suffer the consequences brought about by your rash actions."

The fight rushed back into Karen, and she stepped up onto the riser beside him. "Don't toy with me, David. If this is some kind of joke to get me to withdraw the lawsuit, I'm warning you, I won't be trifled with."

"You are warning me?" His hand gripped the banister so hard his arm shook. "You are the one who is in trouble, lady." He grabbed her by the shoulders, shifting one hand to her chin. He kissed her, fierce and quick. It was over before she could react. "You have your wish, *my dear*. We'll be wed tomorrow afternoon, and I expect this lawsuit to be dropped by the following day." He turned and walked up the stairs every bit as if he saw each one, seemingly in too much of a temper to be tentative.

Karen sank down onto the steps and stared after him, incredulous, her trembling fingers raised to touch her lips, still tingling from his kiss. She remained staring up toward the landing until a door slammed on the second floor. Her bludgeoned mind could hardly take in what had happened. At a noise below her, she turned.

Sam, Jesse, and Matilda crowded in the parlor doorway. Sam rubbed his cheek. "At least Dave's out of his doldrums now."

❧

"What made you change your mind?" Sam plopped into the chair beside the bed and propped his boots on the comforter, making the mattress lurch.

David tucked the fingers of his good hand behind his head and pressed back into the pillow. "General idiocy? Or maybe I thought it would be less expensive to marry her than to go through with that lawsuit."

"Or maybe it's what you want deep down in your heart? You said you still love her."

The memory of Karen's lips under his, even though he'd kissed her in anger, seared David through. He loved her and he wanted her. His abdomen trembled. He knew he was using the lawsuit as an excuse to push past his fears and marry her. But what about later? What about when everything fell apart? "Why did you come up here, Sam?"

"I guess I wanted to make sure. . .I don't know. You know I wouldn't have pushed going through with this wedding if I wasn't one hundred percent sure you two still loved each other, right? If I didn't think it was the best thing for both of you, I never would've gone along with this breach of promise idea."

"How can you say it's for the best? I'm getting railroaded every which way from Sunday. I never would've thought Karen capable of coming up with an idea like this. It's so unlike her. More something Mother would do if she got the bit between her teeth."

Clearing his throat, Sam shifted his weight. "Well, truth be told, the idea did originate with Mother—Now, don't explode. She had the full backing of Father, and Karen just went along with it. You hit it square when you said Mother had the bit between her teeth. And her plan worked, too. You're out of the study, dressed, and things are moving forward for the wedding."

David fisted his hands and pounded his thighs. "You're joking, right? This was all Mother's idea?" And he'd fallen right into it. "I'm such an idiot."

"You aren't going to back out now, are you? Mother will kill me for opening my big mouth. Things are so close to working out between you and Karen. You won't let this upset the ore cart, will you?"

Impotent anger washed over David. He was no more than a rag doll. Without his sight, he couldn't even fight back, falling into the trap Mother had laid for him. And Karen, dancing to Mother's tune, though she didn't bear as much blame since she hadn't known his mother as long as he had. "I won't back out now. I'll give Karen the protection of my name, and she'll be provided for, but don't be fooled into thinking this is some sort of happily-ever-after. Eventually, she'll regret marrying me and she'll leave, or she'll stay and be miserable. And you and Mother and Father will have to live with knowing you pushed us both into this."

Sam tapped him on the leg. "You know, time's going to prove you wrong. When you've been happily married for ten years and have half a dozen kids, I'm going to remind you of this little discussion."

"Stop kidding around. Time isn't going to change the fact that I'm helplessly blind and no fit husband for any woman. This is a legal move, nothing more."

His brother moved to the door. "I'll expect you to name at least one of those kids Sam. See you in the morning, bridegroom."

six

"I don't think I can do this." Karen drew a deep breath, then several more. The bouquet of flowers from the conservatory trembled in her hands.

Jesse leaned down to whisper in her ear. "Don't let my son's sour face fool you. Deep down, he's getting what he wants. Believe it. David loves you and needs you. This is for the best."

She pressed her free hand against the hummingbirds bombarding her stomach.

With little ceremony, Jesse led her into the parlor. Sam stood beside David and ran his finger around his collar as if he was the one getting married. Dear Pastor Van Dyke, his suit rumpled and his white hair running amok, held his Bible before him like a shield. Matilda smiled and nodded encouragement, and beside her, David's cousin Marcus stood. He didn't meet her gaze, and he checked his watch as if he'd rather be anywhere else.

Marcus. He had been one of the first people she'd met when she first got her job at the registry office. She lost count of the times he'd asked her permission to call. Though he was nice enough, she just wasn't interested, especially after meeting David.

She glanced at her soon-to-be husband. He looked like he might try to beat Marcus to the door in a footrace. She blinked back tears. *You're doing the right thing, even if he doesn't realize it right now. Once he learns that your love for him hasn't changed, he'll feel safe showing his love to you. Rome wasn't built in a day, and neither will his confidence return overnight.*

Jesse put her hand into David's, and the ceremony began.

David didn't falter in his vows, though his voice lacked enthusiasm. She repeated her promises, squeezing his hand when she vowed to love, honor, and obey him until death parted them. He gave no indication he felt it.

Pastor Van Dyke pronounced them man and wife. "You may kiss your bride."

Air crowded into her throat. David fumbled for a moment, placed his hand on the side of her face, then kissed her cheek as if she was his mother. She blinked, and the chill that blew through her lingered.

He signed the marriage certificate, his name scrawling off to the side like a primer student's. Karen wrote her name beneath his, swamped with misgivings and doubt one moment, sure she was doing the right thing the next.

Marcus shook David's hand and patted Karen on the shoulder then scooted out the door like his tail was on fire. Karen couldn't blame him, what with David acting like he was taking part in his own execution.

Only once during the wedding breakfast did she catch a glimpse of the David she knew hidden beneath the wounded exterior. Buckford set David's plate before him and leaned down to whisper something Karen didn't catch.

The grim expression cemented on David's face all morning softened, and a smile relaxed his lips. He blew out an easy sigh. "Thank you, Buckford. Thank you for understanding and not judging."

The older man patted David on the shoulder and cast a glance at Karen. If she didn't know better, she'd think Buckford was pleading for understanding himself. She lifted her brows, but he shook his head and returned to the kitchen.

Jesse rose when it came time to serve the wedding cake. "A toast to Karen and David."

Karen lifted her glass of punch. Would David take part?

A trapped breath escaped her chest when he felt for his glass and held it before himself.

"Karen, you are a gracious and lovely addition, and Matilda and I welcome you as the daughter we never had. We know that things don't always work out according to our plans, but they always work out according to God's plan and for our good." He smiled and nodded several times, his eyes suspiciously bright. "David, you've had a bumpy road this past little while, but with Karen by your side, I foresee things smoothing out for you. If I didn't know how much you love each other, I would've suggested waiting for this union, but if ever two people were meant to be together, it's you. I wish you all the happiness you deserve." He raised his glass. "To Karen and David."

Matilda and Sam echoed his words. "Karen and David."

Karen pressed her glass to her lips and took a deep drink, all the while watching David over the rim. He lifted his punch and took a sip, his face thoughtful. Was he softening?

The family scattered as soon as they could decently do so, leaving Karen and David alone together for the first time all day.

She folded her napkin into a square and laid it beside her plate.

"So, what's your next move, Mrs. Mackenzie?"

"I was just going to ask you the same thing. Where do we go from here?"

"You're not already regretting your decision, are you?"

"Of course not. It would be natural for me to ask what your plans are for the near future."

"How appropriate, because I do have plans. Buckford is upstairs packing my things. I'm headed to Denver to take up residence in the town house. Certain information has come to my knowledge that makes it prudent I separate myself from my family for the time being, my mother in particular.

The train departs in two hours."

"You're leaving?" She gripped the napkin, crumpling the precise folds she'd just created. "What about me?"

He rubbed his hand down his face and tested his temple with his fingertips. The bruise had faded to a pale yellowish green, and he didn't wince as he probed. "I can't very well travel alone, now can I?" His lips twisted. "I can't do much of anything alone anymore. You can come along and get a taste of what it means to be married to someone in my condition."

"Why leave your family? And why your mother in particular? I would think you'd prefer to stay here where everything is familiar."

"Suffice it to say, I've had enough of my family pushing me around. Mother can't help herself, and I'd rather you were away from her influence as well. At least if we're in Denver, she won't be dreaming up any wild notions like having her own son sued."

Karen stared at her plate. "You know about that?"

"I know about a lot of things. You've gotten your way about the wedding, you and my mother, but that's as far as I'm willing to go. We're leaving in two hours, so if you're coming, you'd best gather your things."

She swallowed and took a staggering breath. Denver. Perhaps it wasn't such a bad idea. They could be alone, just the two of them in the family's town house. Maybe then some of the barriers to their happiness could begin to come down.

❧

Karen boarded the railcar first, with David following, his hand on her shoulder.

Jesse helped the porter with their bags and hovered in the doorway. "Wallace said to congratulate you on the wedding, and that he's happy he could provide the private railcar for you, especially on such short notice."

Karen stood on tiptoe and kissed her father-in-law's cheek. "Thank him for us. I've never traveled in such luxury before. And thank you for all you and Matilda have done. I'll wire you when we reach Denver, and I'll write every chance I get."

"Be sure you do." Jesse hugged her, his voice gruff. The door slammed in his wake, and Karen stooped to look out the window at his tall frame striding across the platform.

"Alone at last." She unpinned her hat and set it on the table. "It will be nice not to be interrupted for a while. Here, there's a chair just to your right."

David shrugged off her hand and found the back of the chair himself. He removed his overcoat and hat, and once seated, leaned his head back. "We won't be in to Denver until well after dark. I didn't sleep well last night. I'm going to nap." With that he closed his eyes, shutting her out.

She contemplated the transom windows in the high point of the roof. Every time she thought she might have found a way past the armor and walls he'd erected, he cut her off. She dropped onto a velvet upholstered davenport, and her hand fell on the Godey's Lady's Book Matilda had given her. Her mother-in-law had written a letter of introduction to her dressmaker in Denver and instructed Karen to purchase a trousseau and spare no expense. Karen leafed through the pages, but her mind hopped from one thought to another so she couldn't concentrate. Finally she put the book aside to contemplate her husband.

She studied his features, loving each plane and angle of his face. In sleep, his face looked younger, less careworn, relaxed. He had loosened his collar and tie. His watch and fob glinted in the lamplight from the wall sconce.

Jesse had taken the crystal from the watch so David could feel the hands and know the time. His entire family had worked hard to show him they cared, that they loved him and wanted to help him, and yet he'd repelled them at every turn.

"Oh, David," she whispered, "where do we go from here? The more I try to fix what's between us, the more snarled things become."

Conviction whispered through her soul, forcing her to own up to what she hadn't wanted to face. She'd rushed into this marriage, scheming and plotting instead of praying and waiting. Now they were married, and there could be no turning back.

Lord, please forgive me. I have been selfish and willful. Instead of asking for Your will and direction, I rushed ahead, grasping for what I wanted, taking it without waiting for You to give it to me. I'm like Jacob in the Old Testament, conniving to get the blessing rather than waiting for You to give it to me. How can a marriage based upon a scheming plot ever be happy? How can love grow, or how can we glorify You? I am broken, Lord. I beg Your forgiveness and ask You to show me Your will. Help me to love David. Help me to show him Your love.

She wiped at the tears on her cheeks and moved to the desk in the corner. A quick check of the drawer revealed stationery and pen and ink.

Dearest Aunt Hattie,
  There is so much I need to tell you, that I feel a letter can hardly hold it. The first thing you must know is that I am now married.

Karen tried to explain about the accident and David's blindness and thus the quick and quiet wedding. As she wrote, she could almost feel her aunt's arms encircling her. What wouldn't she give to be able to see her aunt now, to petition her for advice?

Hattie had been Karen's lifeline, her only family after her father passed away. Hattie, who had accompanied her brother to the mountains to help him raise his daughter, who had waited until Karen was grown before moving back to Kansas City, her much-loved and much-missed hometown. Perhaps, if Hattie was fully recovered from her illness and back to full strength, she could come to visit them. Maybe for the Christmas holiday.

When David awakened some time later, Karen knew a measure of peace, though she was no closer to knowing how to reach her husband. "Did you have a good nap?"

He rubbed his hands over his face and rolled his shoulders. "Have I slept long?" He reached into his vest pocket and retrieved his watch, his fingers whispering across the face.

"Almost two hours. Are you hungry? A porter brought a tray, but you were sleeping so soundly I didn't wake you."

"I'm not hungry."

"You hardly ate anything at the wedding breakfast. You need something. There's chicken and biscuits and some apple pie." She lifted the cover on a plate. "I had some. It's really good."

"I told you I'm not hungry. Stop hovering."

She replaced the lid and tugged at her lower lip, considering him. "I believe I'll excuse myself for a while. If you change your mind, the tray is on the table beside you. I'll just be down the hall, so if you need me, call out."

"I'm quite capable of sitting here alone without your help, Karen."

Her steps swayed with the movement of the train, and she kept her hand on the wainscoting as she edged down the narrow passageway. She passed a bedroom where a double bed took up almost all the space then another small compartment with two chairs facing one another and a bed folded up into the curve of the ceiling. Beyond that a tiny galley and a washroom.

She splashed water on her face and patted it dry, then took pains to re-pin her hair. When she'd wasted nearly ten minutes, she made her way back to the salon.

He'd eaten at least a little, confirming her suspicion that his proposed lack of hunger was a ruse to avoid eating in front of her. A few biscuit crumbs dotted his vest, but his face was clean.

"This is the most beautiful railcar I've ever been in. There are green velvet drapes and stained-glass transoms overhead. The woodwork—I'm not sure what kind—is stained a honey-gold. And the chairs and davenport are a deep blue. There's a patterned carpet on the floor in greens and blues and golds that harmonizes everything. There's the most cunning little bathroom about four doors along the passage. Though the tub is so small I imagine you'd have to step outside to change your mind."

His hand caressed the armrest of his chair, and his shoe moved slightly, as if picturing in his mind all she said and testing it for himself.

Because he remained silent, she found the courage to continue describing things. "I'm wearing a dark burgundy dress. It has a high-standing lace collar and white cuffs. The skirt is full, probably too full for traveling, but I wore it because you once told me you liked it." She picked up the catalog. "Your mother told me to order some new clothes for the winter season while we're in Denver."

"I'd rather not talk about my mother right now." He stretched his legs out and laced his fingers across his vest. His brows puckered and he brushed the fabric, scattering the few crumbs onto the floor. "I have no idea what I'm wearing. I merely put on what Buckford laid out."

This glimpse into his new dark world set up an ache in her heart. She tried to keep her voice matter-of-fact. "You are wearing gray trousers, a white shirt, and a black silk vest." Her gaze traveled over him, assessing and describing. "Your face is thinner now, and your hair is a bit longer. Only a trace of bruising remains on your temple."

"No one has bothered to describe things for me as you have just done."

Fearful of saying the wrong thing, she tried to put into words what he needed to hear. "Perhaps they didn't know how best to help you. Your family loves you, David. They would do anything for you. They just need to know what." She held her breath for his reaction.

Before he could answer, the train began to slow. A shutter fell over his face, cutting off whatever he had been going to say. His lips formed into a taut line.

She began gathering things and placed David's hat and coat in his hands. "I'll see to a cab and getting our luggage aboard," she said. "Do you want to wait here or in the station?"

"I'll wait here."

A heavy weight sat on her shoulders. He'd been relaxed, almost as if he enjoyed her company, and then he'd reverted to the hurting man hunkering in his shell.

She stepped from the train and scanned the platform. A row of cabs stood lined up at the end of the depot in spite of the late hour. She hailed a driver, and when he'd trotted over to her, beckoned him to retrieve the bags. The conductor walked by, and she gave him the directions Jesse had given her about seeing to parking the private railcar in a siding. Then she turned to get David.

He stood on the railcar platform, hat on his head just so, his coat buttoned. He held the handrail and eased his way down the steps.

She walked over to him and, instead of taking his arm, slipped her hand into the crook of his elbow as she would have if he could see. "This way," she whispered, guiding without being too obvious, she hoped.

❧

David mocked himself for his uselessness when the cabbie

asked Karen for the destination. Shame licked at him that Karen had to see to everything—the cab, the luggage, and the instructions for siding the private car.

Her hand came to rest on his arm, and her body moved against him as she turned in her seat. "David, I don't know the house address."

Realizing now just how much he had disrupted her life, yanking her out of all that was familiar, marrying her in haste, tying her to a blind man who couldn't even walk from the train to a cab alone, he hated himself. He gave the address and sank back into the corner of the cab, inching away from her to cocoon himself in solitude.

The horse's hooves clopped on the hard-packed dirt street. A hurdy-gurdy's tinny melody washed over them as they passed a dance hall, and a tinge of smoke hung in the air. Somewhere someone was cooking cabbage. He tried to envision just where in the city they were and surprised himself when the cab turned when he thought it should. The hooves plopping changed to a clatter as they crossed a wooden bridge. Then the cab rocked to a stop.

"There's a light burning in one of the lower floor windows."

He noticed the relief in her voice. "Father said he sent a telegram to Mrs. Webber to inform her of our arrival."

"Mrs. Webber?"

"The housekeeper." He realized anew how little he'd prepared her for this abrupt uprooting. The house they had planned to build in Martin City this spring would forever stay unbuilt. How could he orchestrate the building when he couldn't see? Yet another piece of his future to throw into the bottom drawer of his mind to molder and decay.

The doorknob rattled. "Is that you, Mr. Mackenzie? Bless me, but come away in. The night's too damp to be standing on the doorstep. And this must be your lovely bride. You could've knocked me down with a gesture when I got your father's telegram."

He pictured the housekeeper as he'd last seen her, gray haired, deep bosomed, motherly, and chatty. "Good evening, Mrs. Webber." His hand hit the iron railing, and he made his way up the steps.

She latched on to his arm and tugged him into the house.

The sounds of footsteps on the walk and the thunk of bags hitting the parquet floor informed him that the baggage had been deposited. Coins clinked, and the cabbie muttered, "Thank ya, ma'am."

Once more his wife had to do tasks that should be his, leaving him sidelined like a toddler in a world of adults.

Karen sighed, as if grateful to have arrived, and the fabric of her dress rustled. He pictured her removing her hat and gloves.

Mrs. Webber's familiar lemon verbena scent surrounded him as she bustled past. "I'll take the bags upstairs." The housekeeper patted his arm again, and he just refrained from brushing her away. "Here you go, missus. You take the lamp and I'll follow you up."

Karen linked her arm through David's. The faint odor of burning kerosene reached him. She stopped him when they reached the upstairs hall and directed him aside.

Mrs. Webber lumbered by with the baggage and deposited it on the carpet.

"Thank you, Mrs. Webber. That's all for tonight."

"Very good, sir. I'll see you in the morning. Sleep well." The housekeeper chortled and coughed, then padded down the stairs humming Mendelssohn's "Wedding March."

❧

Karen's heart lodged somewhere in her throat and beat painfully, making it hard to draw a controlled breath. Her wedding night. She set the lamp on the bureau beside the door and stooped to move the bags so David wouldn't trip on them. "What a lovely room." Did her voice sound as nervous as she felt? "I suppose we can leave most of the unpacking for the morning, don't you?" She crossed to close the navy velvet drapes.

David stood in the doorway. "You can leave my things." He leaned his shoulder on the doorjamb. "Your room is next door. The water closet and bath are across the hall."

She looked at him over her shoulder, her hands gripping the fabric. "My room? But, I thought I would sleep in here. After all, we did get married today."

"That's right. I married you. But this will be a marriage in name only. I have no intention of consummating our union. When the time comes that you realize your mistake in marrying me, you can apply for an annulment."

The air rushed out of her lungs and her head spun. An annulment? "When are you going to understand that I have no intention of leaving you? Did you not hear me today? I promised to love, honor, and obey you until death parted us."

"I heard your promise. Now obey me and take your things to the next room. I'm tired and I'd like to go to bed. It's been a long day." He stepped farther into the room and waited.

Numb at this turn of events, Karen gathered her valise and straightened. "David, can't we talk about this?"

"This is not a matter for discussion. Go to bed."

She gathered the lamp and stepped into the hall. He closed the door behind her, shutting her out as effectively as putting out a cat for the night. The final humiliation came when he turned the key in the lock.

Tears blurred the flame in the lamp she held and smudged the shadowy outline of the carpet runner and the doorways that gaped open like eyeless sockets along the hallway. She went into the bedroom David said was hers and placed the lamp on the dressing table. With chilly fingers she turned up the wick. The furnishings and décor matched the master bedroom exactly.

Her feet sank into the carpet when she crossed to the bed. Cold satin pillowed her body as she lay back across the coverlet. Rejected and humiliated, she tried to make sense of why he would do this to her. Was he punishing her for pushing him into this marriage? And why mention an annulment?

The sobs burning in her throat clamored for release and she gave in, rolling to her side, curling into a ball, and letting go. Nothing had been right between them in such a long time, and now everything was very, very wrong. She had won a victory in forcing him to go through with the wedding, but it was a Pyrrhic victory, indeed.

❧

David rolled over and shucked the blankets twisted about his legs. Karen's sobs had quieted, but that didn't make him feel less a heel. In a moment of weakness he'd let himself be goaded into this marriage against his better judgment. Now he was stuck.

He couldn't, *wouldn't* be her husband in every sense of the word. The possible consequences were too great. Not only might he father a child who might grow to despise his crippled parent, but David knew he would not be able to get that close to Karen, to love her in that way, and then survive when she left him. Better not to give her the chance to hurt him that utterly. Better to keep her at arm's length.

His face flamed at the thought of how inept his attempts at loving would be. He couldn't have borne it if she'd laughed at him or, even worse, pitied his attempts. He would not take that chance, no matter how much he loved her.

She said she loved him right now, but what about later? What about when reality didn't meet up with her fairy-tale expectations and she realized she'd made a mistake? What about when she realized how hard life would be with a cripple who couldn't do the simplest tasks for himself anymore?

His profession was lost to him. Every last shred of who he was and why he existed had vanished. He was dead weight, contributing nothing to the marriage but his name and family fortune. How could he be a husband to her? How could he be the leader in his home, the head of his household?

seven

Light footsteps sounded on the stairs.

The fist of anxiety resting under David's breastbone since Karen left the house early that morning loosened a bit. He hated the idea of his wife roaming the streets of Denver alone, but what could he have done? He was in no position to stop her, nor did he relish the idea of trailing after her through the city as if she were the governess and he the charge to be watched over. At least she'd had the sense to take the carriage.

Fingers tapped on the door.

"Come in." He straightened in his chair and crossed his legs, lacing his fingers in his lap.

When she entered, he schooled his features to appear disinterested and calm. Then her perfume assailed him—light, sweet, beautiful. Just like Karen.

He swallowed. "You were gone a long time."

"Yes, I had lots to do."

"Shopping, I suppose."

"No, actually, I didn't do a bit of shopping, though that's on the list for tomorrow." The fabric of her dress whispered, and her footsteps sounded on the rug.

"What are you doing? Are you pacing?"

"I'm making the bed and tidying your clothes. You didn't go downstairs today, and you didn't let Mrs. Webber in, so the room could use a little looking after." The bedcovers rustled and pillows thumped. The armoire door opened, and the latches on his cases jingled. "You didn't unpack last night, so I'll help you while we talk."

"You sound cheerful." He fisted his hands. Why did it bother him that she did these simple things for him, things the housekeeper would've done?

A drawer slid open. "I am, though I'm tired clear through. I didn't sleep well last night, and I had to go clear across town today."

"What for?" He turned his face toward the sounds of her movement. "And will you stop fussing with my belongings?"

She laughed, and a shaft of pain sliced through him at the musical sound. "Actually, I'm nervous, and I hoped by straightening the room I could buy myself some time to gather my courage before the vials of your wrath fell upon me again."

Though she kept her tone light, he sensed her worry. He timed the sound of her movement, and when she passed close, he reached for her, grasping her wrist. Though a sense of dread at her words formed in his chest, guilt pushed to the forefront of his mind. He didn't want Karen afraid of him, no matter what had happened. "What did you do?"

Her arm twitched, and he realized she had taken a deep breath. "First, I had a chat with Mrs. Webber, and she mentioned the new school for the blind they've just built across town. That's when it hit me. They would be a wealth of information for us. I went straight to the school to find a tutor. A tutor can help us in so many ways. We can make the house easier to navigate and devise some organizational tactics for your wardrobe and office. So many things to make all of this better." Her words rushed out, as if once she started, she wanted to finish without giving him a chance to interrupt.

A protest made it as far as his teeth. He didn't need a tutor. Accepting a tutor meant accepting his blindness. Though the rational part of him knew his blindness was permanent, an unreasoning, fearful part of his heart held on to a shred of hope that this hadn't really happened, that he would wake up one morning and it would all be a bad night that evaporated into a glorious dawn. He would see colors and movement, light and life, and not be shackled in darkness.

"David? Did you hear me?" She knelt before him and placed her hands on his knees.

The warmth of her palms through his pants legs seared him, reminding him of the closeness they had once shared. He shifted and shook his head. "You had no right to interfere this way. A tutor won't change anything. I refuse to have a stranger in the house staring at me and pitying me."

A giggle escaped her lips, making her sound very young. "David, I can guarantee Rex Collison will not stare. He's blind, too."

His thoughts tumbled like water through a sluice. Accepting yet more help, acknowledging again his need for aid, his inability to do the things he used to do. Every moment since he realized he was blind seemed to be proving he was no longer a man.

After an eternity of silence she ventured, "Will you meet Mr. Collison? He's waiting in the parlor. I know he can make things better for you."

"Do you think this will change anything? There is no way you can make this 'all better.' A sightless tutor. A true case of the blind leading the blind. Why can't you leave it alone?" Why couldn't she grasp the fact that his blindness meant the death of her hopes for their future as well? The man she thought to marry, the strong, protecting, professional man she'd fallen in love with didn't exist anymore. That man had died in the bottom of a mine.

She removed her hands, and he derided himself for the feeling of loss her action brought. "David, you have nothing to lose. Just as being blind won't go away, neither will I go away. I won't stop trying to help you. Where is your faith? Where is your courage?"

"When you've walked a mile in my darkness, Karen, perhaps you will have the right to speak to me in such a manner. You know nothing of what it is like to be blind."

"No, I don't know, but Rex does. I should think you'd be willing to at least speak with him."

He could picture her, crossing her arms, her blue eyes, fringed with dark lashes, studying him. The late afternoon sun would caress her hair and a light flush would ride her cheekbones. His feelings for her, carefully leashed, prodded him to acquiesce. "Very well, I will meet him, since nothing else will please you. But remember this. . .I never asked for a tutor. If I so choose, I'll have him out of here before dinner."

She took his arm. "I think you'll like him. He's nearly your age, I would think, and very smart."

"You don't have to sell him to me. I reserve the right to make my own judgment." They navigated the staircase, and David took pains to count the number of steps. Would the shame and regret of his limitations ever dull? His heart rate picked up when they entered the parlor. Hard enough to greet friends and family. Strangers were another ordeal altogether.

"David, this is Rex Collison. Rex, I'm sorry we kept you waiting. I hope Mrs. Webber made you comfortable."

She led David across the room in the area of the fireplace. He could detect the smell of the fire and, when he moved his face to the left, the smell of coffee. "Pleased to meet you."

Something bumped his arm, and he instinctively grasped Collison's hand and shook it.

"I'll leave you to your discussion." Karen squeezed his elbow. "If you'll take a seat, I'll pour some coffee for you and go consult Mrs. Webber about dinner. I hope you'll stay, Rex."

"Thank you. I'd like that."

Her footsteps retreated, leaving them alone.

"Your wife tells me your blindness is recent."

David lifted his cup to his lips and breathed in the warm aroma. "That's right. About five weeks now."

"I hope you took the news better than I did when it happened to me." Rueful amusement tinged Collison's voice. "I was a trial to my family for half a year or more."

David said nothing. Trial he might've been the last month or so, but he wouldn't discuss it with a stranger.

Rex tried again. "I understand you're an engineer."

"Was. I *was*. I'm nothing now."

"On the contrary. You're still an engineer with several years of experience to call upon. There is no reason, with some adaptation to your routine and with a little help from an assistant, why you should cease your work. Your wife told me you have a very capable assistant to call upon."

David set his cup down with more force than he intended, splashing hot liquid onto his hand. "Excuse me, Mr. Collison, but do you have any experience working in a mine? An engineer has to be able to read, to write, to calculate loads, design square sets, gauge the quality of the stope. I cannot work without my eyes."

"In time, you will be able to read Braille and to write in Braille and in script. Your brain wasn't affected by the explosion, only your eyesight. With a competent assistant, your career need not be halted."

For one moment he allowed himself to hope, to believe things might return to the way they had been, but the foolishness of those thoughts crashed down on him. Reality was darkness. Reality was the need to rely on others to help him because he couldn't help himself. Reality was that even before the accident he'd been a bad engineer. Otherwise, the mine never would've caved in. Shame licked through him like greedy tongues of fire, incinerating hope and devouring possibilities.

"My career is dead, and there's nothing I can do about it."

He rested against the antimacassar, wishing he could stop the jangling in his head. Everything he had once identified himself as had been stripped from him, leaving him nothing to hold on to. Had he somehow angered God and earned this judgment? Did God even know or care?

"You won't know what you can do until you try. Think of how the children at the school will admire you and seek to be like you when you prove that even without your sight you are a successful engineer. This will show them there is nothing they might not accomplish if they just try." Collison's chair creaked, as if leaning forward in his zeal to convince David. "You have advantages that many sightless persons do not have. You have the love and support of your family, especially your wife, and you have ample resources at your command. You have a career waiting for you if you have the courage to pick it up again."

David gripped the arms of his chair so hard his hands shook. "I never asked to be a role model."

"You may think I don't understand what you're going through, but I do. Before I became a teacher for the blind, I had just graduated from college. The ink wasn't even dry on my diploma when I fell ill. When the doctors told me I would never see again, I thought it meant saying good-bye to my dreams of teaching." He chuckled. "I never did become the college history professor I wanted to be, but now, looking back, I wouldn't exchange my students at the academy for any cap and gown. God took my dreams and, through a refining fire, made them into something that would glorify Him."

Hot bile rose in David's throat. How much better would it have been if God had seen fit to merely take his life instead of taking his sight? Refining fire. He swallowed, hard. "I think we're finished here for the day." He stalked out of the room and up the stairs, and only when he reached his room and closed the door did he realize he hadn't counted the steps across the foyer or up the staircase.

Karen tipped her head back and blinked to stem the tears blurring her vision. She'd been silly to hang so much hope on the meeting between David and Rex. They had so much in common, and yet David hadn't let Rex past the walls.

She took a firm grip on her emotions and entered the parlor. "Rex"—she sat opposite him—"I'm sorry the interview didn't go well."

He placed his cup on the table at his elbow. A patient smile played around his lips. "I thought it went very well."

"He stormed out like his coattails were on fire. Didn't you hear his door slam?" She smoothed her skirts, then crumpled them again by crunching her hands into the fabric.

"He's dealing with a lot of emotions right now. Anger, bitterness, fear. Overwhelming fear." Rex steepled his fingers under his chin.

"That breaks my heart. David has always been so confident, so sure of himself and his abilities. He had his life planned out, and up until now, his life has gone as he planned."

"That probably makes the situation harder for him to swallow. He's afraid he won't be man enough to face his new circumstances."

"He won't even try, and I can't seem to make him."

Rex inclined his head. "My dear, I hope you'll forgive the familiarity, but I fear you are as much the problem as the solution here."

"What?"

"If I were in David's shoes, I'd be scared stiff myself. According to your housekeeper, you are a strikingly beautiful woman. I'd venture to say you didn't lack for suitors before David claimed you as his fiancée."

Heat tingled in Karen's cheeks, but she didn't interrupt.

She would need to speak to Mrs. Webber about chattering too much while serving guests their tea.

"I can imagine David feels in his heart that he is no longer worthy of such a bride. You told me he tried to break the engagement and that only under pretext of a lawsuit did he go through with the ceremony. I suspect it was less the lawsuit than the fact that he couldn't bear the thought of your walking out of his life that made him marry you. I would suspect he is terrified you will wake up one day and realize you've made a mistake, that you regret marrying him."

"I would never." She spoke through stiff lips and clenched teeth, her hands fisted in her lap. "I love David, blind or not, though he's testing my patience to the limit."

Rex laughed, putting his hands up in surrender. "I believe you. I'm just trying to help you understand things from David's perspective. I think, in time, he'll come to trust that your love for him hasn't changed. It's the time before that will be difficult. You're going to need all your patience and wisdom to withstand the coming storm. I speak from experience, both as a man who was blinded as an adult and as a teacher who has encountered many a troubled student. Things are likely to get worse before they get better."

Karen rubbed her temples. "I can't imagine their getting worse. I barely know myself anymore. My feelings are all jumbled up. On the one hand I want to cry and comfort him and help him heal, and on the other I want to throw something and stomp my foot and scream at him for ruining what is supposed to be one of the best times of our lives. We've had no honeymoon, and the newlywed phase of our marriage has been less than cordial." Her voice cracked. A tear trickled down her cheek, and she scrubbed it away, mortified to have broken down in front of a guest, a man she barely knew.

Rex reached out a searching hand and awkwardly patted

her arm. "I'm sorry. I will do all I can to help both of you, but you'll have to be patient. Nothing will change overnight. Much like he's done with me, David hasn't sent you away, so he must want you here. Cling to that hope and try not to brood. You'll feel better if you stay busy."

"What can I do?"

"There are several practical things we prescribe for all our students, and you can get started on those now—things like labeling his clothing and organizing his possessions. When I get back to the school, I'll talk things over with our headmaster, Mr. Standish, and together we'll come up with a plan."

He rose and his ever-ready smile encouraged her. "Don't worry. I've handled tough cases before. David didn't expressly forbid me to return tomorrow, so I'll be here in the morning. We'll continue his first lessons here at the house, but eventually, I'd like him to come to the school. The students would benefit from meeting him when he's gotten over the worst of things, and there are some resources there that would be helpful."

eight

Karen snipped her thread and ran her thumb over the bumps. She rechecked the notes Rex had given her, making sure the small French knots were in the right positions to represent the colors. Something else to cross off her list.

Along with reorganizing his wardrobe and toiletries, she and Mrs. Webber had removed nearly half the furnishings from the parlor. Though current fashion leaned toward dozens of occasional tables, tightly packed chairs and settees, and bric-a-brac on every surface, Karen had to admit she liked the sparse look to the room now. David had said nothing of the changes, but he moved with more confidence now that he didn't have to circumnavigate so many obstacles.

A Braille book sat on the desk across the parlor. David had yet to pick it up on his own, though he had allowed Rex to return every day this week for lessons. Karen rejoiced in this small success, but Rex's prediction that changes would come slowly was proving all too depressingly true. At the moment the pair was in the dining room, where they had spent the majority of the last two days.

Mrs. Webber appeared in the doorway. "Ma'am, there's a fellow here to see you, says he's the butler." A scowl marred the housekeeper's normally sunny face. She stepped back and revealed Buckford standing in the foyer. "I didn't know you'd hired a butler."

"Buckford." Karen rose, letting the shirt drop onto her sewing basket. "What are you doing here?" The sight of his familiar face, so comforting and bracing, caused tears to prick Karen's eyes. The older man had a box under one arm and a valise under the other. "Did you walk from the station?" Red suffused his nose and cheeks, and a wintry air perfumed his coat. "Did Mr. and Mrs. Mackenzie come with you?"

"Yes ma'am, I did walk, and no ma'am, the family is not with me. Mrs. Mackenzie thought I might be of some help to you. She sends her regards and this letter." He set his bag down and fished in his coat pocket.

"I can't wait to read it. You don't mind if I take a peek now, do you?" Karen tore the envelope open with eager fingers. She scanned the page, letting the comforting words seep into the lonely places in her heart.

Dear Karen,

I've had to resist boarding the train to Denver every day since you left, so great is my desire to come to you and to ascertain how you are coping. Since I know this wouldn't be prudent, I've done the next best thing and sent Buckford. He and David have always shared a close bond, and perhaps Buckford will be a comfort to you and a help.

I hope you've taken me at my word to acquire a new wardrobe for the winter. Bill everything to the Mackenzie accounts and spare no expense. There was no time to assemble a trousseau for you, so consider this a wedding gift.

I know you weren't keen on the idea of the lawsuit, and in retrospect perhaps it wasn't the best idea, but the truth is, I was at the end of my rope. I love my son, but he has inherited all my stubbornness and a fair dose of his father's as well. He had bested all my efforts, and I was not of a mind to let him continue in his current path of action. Though the end result, the wedding, was what I was after, having talked things over with Reverend Van Dyke, he has reminded me that the ends don't justify the means. If I pushed you beyond what you were comfortable with, I apologize. I can be quite headstrong, as you know. David gets that from me.

All I can advise with David is that you keep your generously loving heart open to him. With you working on the outside and God's Spirit working on the inside, his heart will heal. I knew such joy when you two first began courting because you loved David so much. That love and God's strength will bring you through.

Know that I am lifting you both up daily, even hourly, in prayer, and know that you can call upon us for anything you need.

Love,
Matilda

Warmth at her mother-in-law's thoughtfulness bathed Karen, and she looked up through watery eyes at Buckford. "I don't know how they'll get along without you in Martin City, but I can't tell you how glad I am that you're here." There were so many things that David wouldn't allow Karen to help him with but that Buckford could do without undue embarrassment to his employer.

"Mr. Sam sent this box of papers and ore samples and a letter for Mr. David." He picked up his satchel.

She nibbled her lower lip. "Mrs. Webber, show Buckford to the room at the end of the hall."

"Yes, ma'am." The housekeeper's narrowed eyes continued to travel up and down Buckford's frame, sizing him up.

Buckford rejoined Karen in the parlor a few moments later. "How may I best assist you, ma'am?"

"David is in the dining room with his tutor, Rex Collison. The box you brought can go in the upstairs office. I don't think David should be bothered with anything from the mine right now. He's concentrating on his new studies."

"Very good, ma'am. Then perhaps it would be politic to go smooth Mrs. Webber's ruffled feathers. I'll reassure her that I have no intention of usurping her place here."

"Thank you, Buckford. You're very astute."

Karen packed her sewing basket, then took a moment to read again her mother-in-law's letter. Love David generously. If only he would let her. She took the precious pages upstairs, along with an armful of David's clothes.

When she came downstairs a short time later, David and Rex stood in the foyer.

Buckford appeared from the back of the house. "Good afternoon, sir."

"Buckford?" David's voice went high. His eyebrows arched, then tumbled. "What are you doing here?" He stuck his hand out, and Buckford clasped it.

"Your mother thought I might be of use to you."

"I'm glad you're here." The warmth in his tone reminded Karen of how much regard David had for Buckford. She quashed a bit of jealousy that her husband was more comfortable with his hired man than with his wife.

"Gentlemen"—she walked down the last few stairs—"I hope your lessons went well today." She slipped her hand into the crook of David's elbow.

A smile crossed Rex's face, but David stiffened as if she'd jabbed him in the ribs. When he didn't say anything, Rex offered, "Very well, thank you."

"Can you stay to dinner, Rex? We'd love to have you. Mrs. Webber's making her specialty, beef Wellington. It should be ready soon."

"I wish I could, but I'm expected back at the school. David, I'll be back tomorrow morning. I'll also expect a report of how tonight goes."

Her hand must've tightened, because David shifted. "Rex expects me to dine at the table tonight. I hope that meets with your approval."

"Really? That's wonderful." She shared a smile with Buckford. "I shall enjoy your company." She prayed that perhaps he might enjoy hers as well.

❧

Mrs. Webber announced dinner just as David closed the door on Rex's departure.

Karen tucked her hand into his arm once more, sending a jolt through him and making his heart hammer. As loath as he was to admit it, the idea of dinner with Karen brought a curious lightness to his chest, a faint echo of the way he'd felt when he first began courting her.

She waited beside him, her light perfume drifting around him. Her skirts rustled in a purely feminine sound. How he wished he could see her face, her hair in the candlelight, her graceful walk.

He took a deep breath. "Shall we go in?" He called down thankfulness upon Rex's head for making him practice seating a lady at the table, though he was sure Mrs. Webber had grown weary of the exercise before he'd finally mastered it. When Rex suggested Karen take part in the practice, David's reply had been curt and decisive. He might bumble in front of the housekeeper, but he would not appear a clumsy oaf in front of his wife.

"Thank you, David."

A thrust of pride shot through him at the surprise in her voice, and he exhaled a tight breath when he managed to push her chair in without mishap. He sat at her left hand and lightly fingered the silverware and goblet placement, trying to force his muscles to relax.

Mrs. Webber placed his plate in front of him. The china clinked as she rotated it to the correct position. "There you are. Ring when you want dessert."

He spread his napkin in his lap and picked up his knife and fork. *Small bites, slowly, main course at twelve, sides at four and eight. Let your fork hang over the plate for a count of three. Lean over.* Rex's instructions cycled through his head in a continuous loop. He held the fork lightly, focusing on the sensations coming from the tines to his fingers.

"I was so surprised when Buckford showed up." Karen's utensils clinked against her plate, and her sleeve whispered on the tablecloth.

David moved his fork to his mouth, pleased when nothing dripped down his chin. The flavor of beef and gravy burst on his tongue. "Good of Mother to send him."

Silence fell. When first courting, they had spent hours talking. Time had flown when they were together, and it had seemed they would never run out of things to say to one another. He'd wanted to know everything about her and tell her everything about himself. Now they sat like strangers. No. Worse than strangers. Strangers would at least make small talk.

His skin prickled and tightened. She watched him— he could feel her appraisal. How clumsy he must look to her, like a tentative toddler. His fork clattered to his plate, sending droplets of warm gravy across his face. When he scrambled to retrieve the fork, the heel of his hand hit his plate and dumped the contents into his lap.

"Oh, no." Her chair shot back, and before he could move, wet cloth dabbed his face. "Hold still."

He writhed away from her, shoving the napkin aside. "Don't." In his effort to get away, he knocked her arm.

She gasped an instant before cold liquid bathed his chest. Something thumped on the carpet. "I'm so sorry." She mopped at his shirtfront. "I had my water glass in my hand to dampen my napkin and I dropped it."

He gritted his teeth, grabbed her wrists, and shoved his chair back. "Stop, Karen. I should've known better than to try this. I'm a clumsy fool and always will be." The warmth of her skin in his grasp, the heady aroma of her perfume swirling around him, the soft sound of her breathing all taunted him. "Why did you ever marry me? Can't you see this was all a mistake? I'm inept at even the simplest task. I'm not a man. I'm a liability." He stumbled against the table, rattling the china, and made his way out of the room.

≈

Karen sank into her chair and put her elbows on the table. She rested her face in her hands, utter weariness cloaking her, pressing her shoulders down and squeezing her heart. Why did it seem that for every inch of hard-won progress David made, a stumbling block tripped him up and yanked him back toward a yawning chasm of despondence?

"Lord," she whispered, "I don't know what to do. I can't get close to him. He won't let me help him. The more I press, the faster he retreats." She swallowed against the spiky lump in her throat and took a staggering breath. She needed to find something positive, something to be thankful for, to gain some equilibrium. "Thank you for Rex. Thank you that David is at least willing to listen to him."

She sat quiet for a while, calming her heart, letting God's peace return. "Please, Lord, help me to be patient. Help me not to be jealous that David is turning to Rex or Buckford for help when he won't turn to me. Help me to rely on You for direction, and please, break down the barriers around his heart. Help him to forgive himself and to accept his blindness. Please help him to accept his marriage as well." Karen leaned back and put her hands in her lap. She blinked rapidly, bringing the plaster medallion on the ceiling into focus.

"Missus?" Mrs. Webber hovered in the doorway. "Should I bring in dessert?"

Karen pushed her plate back and rose. "I'm sorry, Mrs. Webber. The dinner was delicious, but I think we'll save dessert for tomorrow. If you could just clear away. David has retired for the night, and I think I will, too."

The housekeeper's eyes shone with sympathy as she took in the splattered tablecloth and the water glass on the floor. "The poor creature." She clucked, shook her head, and began stacking plates and cutlery.

Karen didn't know if "poor creature" meant her or David.

nine

"This is ludicrous." David slammed the book closed and tilted his head back against his chair. Nothing had gone right the entire week, not since his disastrous dinner with Karen.

"David, you just have to be patient." Rex's soothing tone rasped on David's nerves. "It will take time, but you're making progress."

"Don't patronize me. Braille is beyond me. I can't do this."

"I think what you really mean to say is you don't want to *have* to do this." Rex slapped the desk. "I think it's time someone told you a few home truths. You say to stop treating you like a child, but your actions are childish. You haven't accepted your blindness. You will never be free to learn until you accept the fact you are blind and destined to stay that way."

Rex rose, and the direction of his voice told David he was leaning over the desk. "Do you think you are the only one to ever go through something like this? Do you think you are the only one in this house who is suffering? Stop for just a moment and think how this is affecting someone else. I may not be able to see, but I'm not stupid. I haven't heard you say one kind or affectionate thing to your wife since I arrived in this house. You speak better to your servant or to me, a virtual stranger, than you do to the woman you married. You are so swamped with fear, you aren't just blind. You're emotionally paralyzed."

He wanted to squirm. Rex had no business hitting so close to the truth. "You know nothing of the situation, and I'll thank you to keep your nose out of it."

Rex gave a short bark of laughter, all traces of patience and understanding gone. "You think I don't know what you are going through? I wasn't born blind, David. I was a college graduate with dreams of becoming a teacher and eventually a professor of history. I had prospects in the academic field, a fiancée, a future all mapped out. Then, in the space of a few weeks' illness, I had nothing. My fiancée couldn't face marrying a blind man and fled. My teaching job ended before it got started, and for a while, I thought even God had abandoned me. I now know He was there all the time, watching over me, guiding me, healing my hurts. Though I couldn't see with my physical eyes, God brought new sight to my spiritual eyes. He had better things in store for me, and I would have missed them if not for the blindness."

"Better things?" Bitterness coated David's tongue. "How can blindness be better than sight? You lost your job, your girl, and your independence."

Rex's chair creaked and his voice moderated. "While I was busy making plans for my life, I never once considered if those plans were God's will or if I would be serving Him by being a college professor. I wanted the recognition and the status of teaching at a university someday. I was so full of my own plans and desires I left God completely out of the equation. God had a better plan for me. I lost a girl who wouldn't stick by me when I became blind. I'm just thankful I found it out before we were actually married. I'm now engaged to a wonderful, godly young woman I met at the academy. And before you say, 'Of course, one blind person marrying another. What else can you expect?' I'll tell you she's not blind. Her father, Mr. Standish, runs the school, and my Aimee loves God and loves me enough that my blindness doesn't matter to her a bit. As for losing my independence, isn't that what God wants most for us as His children? God doesn't want us to be independent. He wants us to be totally dependent on Him. Without Him, even men with perfect vision are blind."

David snorted his disbelief. "I prefer to think that God helps those who help themselves, and I can't very well help myself now, can I?"

"You realize that little homily isn't even in the Bible? When I met with your wife about taking this job, she said you were a Christian struggling with God over your blindness. It was one of the reasons I was willing to take this job. I thought I could help you, because I struggled, too."

David put his elbows on the desk and slid his fingers into his hair. "I don't want to talk about this anymore."

"I know you don't, but you can't continue as you are. I know how exhausting it can be running from God. You won't have any peace until you realize there is nowhere you can go to get away from Him. He will pursue you with His love to the ends of the earth or the depths of your despair. Give up on the bitterness and the running away, David, or it will consume you. It will ruin your relationship with God, your marriage, and your career."

"All of that is ruined already." His chest ached. "I have nothing left."

"I'll be the first to admit things won't ever be as they once were for you, but you're selling yourself short if you think you have nothing left to offer anyone."

David's heart smoldered. It was galling for a man of his education and accomplishments to be forced to begin his schooling over again like the smallest primary student. To learn his letters at his age. No matter how proficient he became at reading those exasperating bumps on the page, he would never be able to work in the mine office again. It was like a death to him, the loss of his career. He *was* an engineer. All his adult life he'd been identified by that term. He sought elusive ore, directing an army of miners to find hidden treasure. David Mackenzie was an engineer. Was. . . Was. . . Was. . .

Rex opened the book before him. "Shall we begin again?"

He sighed, placed his fingertips on the paper, and settled them along the top row. Before he could once again begin sounding out the words, the door opened.

She was home. He knew it was her before she even spoke. Every day this week his wife had gone shopping, leaving the house early, lunching uptown, and coming home in the late afternoon. A swirl of chilly air accompanied her entrance into the parlor, and the smell of snow vied with her perfume. He envisioned her shrugging out of her coat and tugging off her gloves.

David pushed back his chair and rose a fraction of a second after Rex's chair scraped the floor.

"Good afternoon, gentlemen. How are the lessons going?"

"I think we've done enough for the day. I'll be taking my leave." Rex closed his book. "David, we'll meet again tonight? I hope you'll consider carefully what we discussed this afternoon."

"Tonight?" Karen asked. "What's happening tonight, David?"

"There's a program at the school tonight, recitations and such. To raise funds, I gather. Rex could explain it better. In a weak moment I promised we'd attend."

"You're leaving the house? That's wonderful. We haven't had a night out in ages."

The excitement in her voice made David purse his lips. When they were courting, they'd attended every production at the Martin City opera house. Several times over the past few weeks, she'd asked him if he would like to go to the symphony or to a play. Each time he had declined, a fine sweat breaking on his skin at the thought of going out in public, having to meet new people he couldn't see. He could barely navigate his own house. How could he escort his wife to a public function? The only saving grace about tonight's affair was that it would take place at the blind school where most of the people wouldn't be gawking.

❧

Karen gave her reflection a cheeky wink and scooped up her new cloak. For the first time in her month-old marriage, she and her husband would be doing something normal—going out for the evening.

Her heart tripped as lightly as her feet on the way down the stairs. She'd mulled over everything Rex had said about David's fears and why he was having such a difficult time adjusting to his blindness, putting it together with David's own comment about being a liability. She'd have to prove to him over time that she had no intention of leaving him and pray that as he studied and worked with Rex his confidence in his abilities would return. Until that day, she would take each hurdle as it came. As for tonight, she planned to enjoy herself.

David waited in the foyer. The sight of him in evening dress made her breath hitch. So handsome with his broad shoulders, fine features, and strong personality, no man had ever come close to him in her estimation. She bit her lip and steadied herself.

Be yourself. Act as you would if the accident had never happened.

"Good evening, David." Before she could talk herself out of it, she walked to his side, put her hand on his arm for balance, and rose on tiptoe to place a kiss on his cheek. "You look so handsome tonight. Would you help me with my cloak?" She handed it to him before he could refuse and turned her back.

He was still for a moment. Finally, he placed his hand on her shoulder, sending warm, golden arrows through her, and, only fumbling a little, settled the garment about her.

She tugged on her gloves and threaded her arm through his. "It's a beautiful night, and the stars are out." She waited for him to close the front door and escort her down the steps.

He kept one hand on the rail and hesitated with each step, but he got her to the curb without mishap.

She smiled. Much better than when they'd first arrived in

Denver when he'd stood to the side and waited on her to guide him everywhere.

He handed her up into the carriage and settled in beside her. With a lurch, they were off.

"It's been so long since we had an outing. It feels nice to dress up and go somewhere together."

"It must be a bit boring for you, staying in every night." He ran his fingertips along the windowsill and down the side of the carriage.

"I miss my friends in Martin City, though your mother is so good about writing to me. I'm sure once word gets out that we've gone to one event, there will be invitations to parties and gatherings. We've already received one for a Christmas dinner and dance at the Windsor in a few weeks." The invitation sat on the mantel. She hadn't told him about it until now, hoping for some indication that he might be adjusting to his new circumstances before asking him if they could go.

"A trip to the blind school is one thing, a party at the Windsor something else altogether. I'm not going to mingle with Denver society to be stared at and gossiped about."

"Even if they did, wouldn't it be just a nine days' wonder? When they saw how you haven't really changed, that you're still the same handsome, intelligent man you always were, wouldn't they find something else to talk about?"

A chuckle escaped him, and for a moment she thought he might relent. "Flattery won't change my mind, Karen. I'm not opening myself up to their speculation. No parties."

She blew out a breath and tried not to be disappointed. "Then I'll have to make the most of tonight, then. I'm glad the dressmaker had my things finished so I could wear a new gown. A new dress always makes an evening special."

"I suspect my bank account will feel the weight of today's plunder."

The coach lamp hanging just outside the door outlined his

profile in soft, gold light. A smile played around his lips, as if he didn't particularly mind the expense.

"Actually, my trousseau is a wedding gift from your parents. Wasn't that nice of them?" She took his hand and placed it on her sleeve. "Feel. It's indigo silk with beaded trim, and the cloak is black velvet." She picked up the edge of her cloak and brushed it across the backs of his fingers.

A curious softness came over his expression, and his eyes narrowed ever so slightly, as if concentrating. "I told the dressmaker that each dress needed to be of a different fabric. Moiré taffeta, linen, wool, brocade satin. . ."

"Why such variety?"

She swallowed, hoping he would understand. "If each dress has a different feel, then you'll know what I'm wearing without having to ask. I wanted each outfit to have a unique texture for you." A laugh at herself bubbled up. "I know men don't think about such things as what their wives wear, but it was something small I could do for you." She tucked her hand inside his.

As if he couldn't help it, his fingers closed around hers, nestling her hand in his like a bird.

Tears pricked her eyes as she studied his face, waiting, praying for some response.

He pressed his lips together and his throat lurched. "That was very thoughtful of you." The low, husky quality of his voice sent shivers up her spine. "Thank you."

The coach swung into the semicircular drive in front of the school. Karen couldn't help but hope that perhaps they'd turned a corner in their journey together.

ten

Different fabric for each dress? David marveled at her ingenuity, and her generosity humbled and shamed him. Would he, in her place, have been as thoughtful?

Her hand in his felt right, and he hadn't missed her subtle demands on him to behave as a gentleman regarding opening doors and helping with wraps. And he'd surprised himself by accomplishing those tasks without mishap.

He touched his cheek where he could still feel the brush of her lips and the whisper of her breath against his skin. The delicate scent of her perfume wrapped around him.

When the coach lurched to a halt, he almost bolted out the door. Remembering his manners, he stopped and held out his hand to help her.

When she stood beside him on the sidewalk, she tucked her hand into his elbow and gave him a squeeze. "I'm so glad Rex talked you into coming tonight."

Guilt pricked him. Karen was young and beautiful, full of life. She deserved to go to parties and plays, the opera or the symphony. He blew out a breath. Would her departure take place in stages? Would she start going to those places without him? Would he try to stop her?

"There are six stairs up to a stoop." Karen waited for him to take the first step. "The building is brick, three stories, and every window is lit. Very welcoming."

Piano music provided background to what sounded like a hundred different conversations. "How many people are here?" Apprehension feathered across his chest. He shrugged out of his coat when someone asked for it, then turned to help Karen with her wrap.

"Rex, good evening." Her voice held genuine warmth.

Rex introduced his fiancée. Aimee had a pleasant contralto voice that took on a special quality when she spoke to Rex. David recognized the proud and proprietary tone of Rex's voice.

Karen took David's arm. "We're in the foyer, and there are paper chains everywhere for decorations. The party is being held in a room to our left. It looks like it might be the school dining room. Chairs have been arranged in rows, and there must be about sixty adults here."

With subtle pressure, Karen directed him through the room. "We're following Rex and Aimee to where the headmaster and his wife are greeting guests."

Rex introduced everyone and directed them to the seats he'd reserved.

Mr. Standish had a firm handshake. "Good to meet you, David. Rex is treating you well, I hope?"

David forced himself to smile. "Better than I deserve, most likely. During this afternoon's lesson, I was prepared to hurl a book across the room, but he talked me out of it."

Standish steered him to a chair, talking all the while. "Ha, I can imagine. Do you know how many books I had to dodge when teaching Rex?"

David took the chair and eased himself into it. With half an ear he listened to Karen and Aimee chattering about dresses and the decorations. He tried to get a sense of the room, of the space, by listening. The ceiling must be high overhead, and he had a sense of space before him. Karen sat on one side, with Mr. Standish on the other.

"You're in the front row, David." Mr. Standish leaned in. "This room doubles as both dining room and assembly hall. With only two dozen students at the moment, there's plenty of room to grow."

With the way Standish could read people, he must be a good headmaster. David settled back and categorized the sounds and smells around him. Furniture polish, books, boiled potatoes, chalk, and soap. Laughter, conversation, the squeak of a chair as someone shifted his weight, a nervous giggle from a young person.

Rex's voice came from in front and above him, on the stage. "Good evening and welcome. Thank you all for coming to our evening of recitation."

The crowd stilled.

"Our first student tonight is Charles Barrow who will be reciting Psalm 139."

Polite applause rippled through the crowd, and Karen tucked her hand into his.

She'd done that several times this evening, and he had to admit he liked it, even while he reproached himself for those feelings. Each crack he allowed in his armor would only mean more pain when she left him.

"O Lord, thou hast searched me, and known me."

The student must be about ten or so, his voice still pitched high. Had he been blind since birth? Would that be better or worse?

"I will praise thee; for I am fearfully and wonderfully made: marvellous are thy works; and that my soul knoweth right well. My substance was not hid from thee, when I was made in secret, and curiously wrought in the lowest parts of the earth. Thine eyes did see my substance, yet being unperfect; and in thy book all my members were written, which in continuance were fashioned, when as yet there was none of them."

Fearfully and wonderfully made? Maybe once upon a time, but now, ruined as he was, David couldn't imagine those words pertaining to himself.

"Whither shall I go from thy spirit? or whither shall I flee from thy presence? If I ascend up into heaven, thou art there:

if I make my bed in hell, behold, thou art there. If I take the wings of the morning, and dwell in the uttermost parts of the sea; even there shall thy hand lead me, and thy right hand shall hold me."

David's neck muscles tightened and his throat constricted. How long had it been since he felt God's presence?

"If I say, Surely the darkness shall cover me; even the night shall be light about me. Yea, the darkness hideth not from thee; but the night shineth as the day: the darkness and the light are both alike to thee."

The night shining as day? Dark and light might be the same to God, but everything was darkness to David now, as if he were imprisoned in the deepest mine shaft. God had stolen everything David treasured, then left him alone in the dark.

Karen's hand moved in his. He loosened his grip, only now aware of how hard he'd been squeezing her fingers. She rubbed small circles on the back of his hand.

"Search me, O God, and know my heart: try me, and know my thoughts: And see if there be any wicked way in me, and lead me in the way everlasting."

David heard little of the rest of the recitations. His thoughts behaved like ball bearings dropped on a hard floor. He chased first one, then another, never able to line them up squarely.

What had gone wrong at the mine? What should he have done differently? Why had Karen married him when he was so obviously flawed? Would he ever master Braille, and what difference would it make if he did? Why was God so far away? Was his blindness a punishment from God for being so careless at the mine?

Not until Karen stirred beside him did he realize the program had ended. They filed out, her hand under his arm. He forced his face into a pleasant expression and let her steer him toward the side of the immense room.

She stood on tiptoe and whispered into his ear, "There's a

donation table by the door." A tinge of doubt flavored her tone.

He pressed his lips together. Before leaving the town house he'd tucked his wallet into his inner coat pocket. Though it seemed strange, for now he couldn't tell a five-dollar bill from a fifty. He withdrew the leather wallet and handed it to her. "There are blank checks in there. Write one out for a hundred dollars."

"Thank you, David."

He could hear the smile in her voice and warmth spread through him. "They deserve it. Rex has been very patient with me."

The only awkward moment before their departure came when he had to sign the check. "They have a fountain pen. You'll do fine." She spread the slip for him and positioned his hand. "You've signed your name a thousand times."

The pen scratched on the paper.

She picked the check up, and it rustled as she waved it to dry the ink. "Perfect."

He declined the finger sandwiches and asked only for a half cup of punch to minimize what he could spill.

Karen stayed by his side, but he didn't sense she was hovering or afraid to leave him alone. It seemed she took every opportunity to touch him, smoothing his lapel, taking his arm, letting her fingers brush his.

Almost before he was ready, they were back in the carriage headed home.

Karen yawned and laid her head on his shoulder. "Thank you for taking me out tonight. I had a wonderful time. You seemed to enjoy yourself. Did you have a good time?"

"I did."

She laughed. "Don't sound so surprised. I can't believe how much scripture those children had memorized. Did you have a favorite?"

"The first one, I suppose."

"That was my favorite, too. Can you imagine? God knew everything about us before we were even born. There's nowhere we can hide from Him and nowhere that His love can't reach us." She sighed and rubbed her cheek against his topcoat. "I find that very comforting, don't you?"

What he found comforting was having her so close to him. In the close confines of the carriage, with the success of the evening behind them and with her head on his shoulder, he almost felt as if he were a whole man. The longings her touch had fired repeatedly throughout the evening overwhelmed him once more. He turned to her, took her face between his palms, and ran his thumb across her lips. Gardenias perfumed her hair, and the smooth, satin lining of her hood tickled the backs of his hands, reminding him of her thoughtful choice of wardrobe.

Her pulse thrummed along her neck, and her breath caught in a soft pant that made his heart thunder. Before he could stop himself, he lowered his lips to hers.

The kiss went straight to his head, familiar and unknown all at the same time. Softer than her velvet cloak, warmer than a fireside in winter, more comforting than an embrace, and more exciting than a runaway train. He was transported, carried out of his misery into a peaceful place where only they existed. He freed her lips and trailed feathery kisses along her jaw and temple, trying to catch his breath.

Then he opened his eyes, fully expecting to see her face, to see the love shining there.

Darkness.

Reality doused him like ice water. He eased back, swallowing, trying to moisten his suddenly dry mouth. His defenses had lowered for only a moment, and he'd been swept away. Doubts swamped him, and all the reasons he needed to keep her at arm's length surged back.

"David?" She leaned into him again and cupped his cheek.

He captured her hand and set it in her lap. "No. No more. You don't know what you're doing."

"I know that I love you. I know that we're married." She cupped his cheek again.

He reached up and took her hand, placing it in her lap once more. "No, Karen." He turned away from her and tried to gather his scattered wits. How would he survive when she left him? One kiss and he was undone.

eleven

The carriage lurched to a halt, and Karen wiped her damp cheeks, gathering her cloak around her.

David helped her descend from the carriage but released her hand quickly.

The clock in the parlor chimed as they entered.

Buckford held the door, taking their outer wraps as they shed them. His keen eyes searched her face, and she gave him a rather watery smile and a small shrug. He pursed his mouth and leveled a stare at David, shaking his head.

"Sir, you have a visitor in the parlor. She insisted on waiting, though I told her you'd be quite late."

"A visitor? At this hour?" David stopped on the bottom stair, one hand on the newel post.

"A Mrs. Patrick Doolin. She said she'd come all the way from Martin City and had to see you tonight."

David flinched. His shoulders slumped, and he rubbed the back of his neck.

"David? Who is Mrs. Doolin? Do you know her?"

"We've met. Her husband used to work for Mackenzie Mining. He died in the cave-in."

The breath Karen took skidded in her throat. Still rocking from his kiss and being pushed away, she had no strength left for a visitor, especially one with a grievance against the Mackenzies. But what else could they do? "Thank you, Buckford. David, let's get this over with."

Buckford had stirred up the fire, and a tea tray sat on a low table beside the woman. Dressed in black from head to foot, her brown hair streaked with gray, she had a careworn and lined face.

"Mrs. Doolin? I'm Karen Mackenzie. I'm sorry you had to wait so long." Karen held out her hand.

Like a bird, the woman hopped out of the chair and bobbed her head. "I'm the one who should be apologizing, barging in on you. I'll be real quick-like and leave you in peace." Her brogue was as thick as Irish stew. The woman's black, lively eyes darted a look over Karen's shoulder to David. "Mr. Mackenzie, 'tis me, Maggie Doolin."

"Mrs. Doolin." David inched forward until his hand brushed the edge of the desk. Deep lines formed on his forehead, the flickering firelight accenting the creases.

"Please, Mrs. Doolin, do sit down. What is it you've come to talk to my husband about?" Karen took the chair next to their visitor's.

David leaned against the edge of the desk and crossed his arms as if bracing himself for a barrage.

The lines on Mrs. Doolin's face spoke of years of hardship, but peace shone from her dark eyes. Her fingers kept up constant motion, picking at a thread, tapping her lap, never still. "I'm on me way back East, and I had something to say to my late husband's boss. I should have come before, but I was making ready to return to me family. Me oldest boy lives in Boston. He's asked me to come to him now that I'm alone."

Karen leaned forward. "We're so sorry for your loss."

"Aye, lass, I know you are. 'Tis a terrible thing for the women, isn't it, waiting to see if our men will come back out of the earth when they search for buried treasures? You haven't escaped the sorrow yourself. I'm that sorry about Mr. Mackenzie's eyes. My Paddy thought the world of Mr. Mackenzie, he did. And he was that proud of his dynamiting. An artist he was. The best powder monkey in the silver fields." She dug a handkerchief out of her sleeve, using it to wipe the corners of her eyes. After a moment, she gathered herself. "'Twas about Paddy I've come, Mr. Mackenzie."

David grimaced. "I'm so sorry, Mrs. Doolin. I hope you can believe that. I have no excuses to offer. The structure I designed failed in some way. I know there's no recompense I can make that will replace what you've lost, but I do hope you understand that you will be provided for. You've spoken to my father or brother?"

"Oh, now, don'tcha be worried, sir. I didn't come to bother you. Paddy wouldn't have blamed you, and neither do I. Your family's been very generous. Your lady-mother herself came to see me. I've no quarrel with Mackenzie Mining. I came to tell you what Paddy said to me afore he died. He lingered two days after they dug him out of the rubble. The doc couldn't do anything for his broken back, though 'twas God's mercy my Paddy could feel no pain. When he knew he was dying, he held my hand that hard and made me promise on me mother's grave I'd tell you his last words."

David's knuckles showed white.

Karen wanted to go to him, to put her arms around him and offer some comfort, but she couldn't bear to be rebuffed in front of a guest.

"What is it your husband wanted to tell me?"

"Paddy was pretty far gone, so I don't know if I heard him right, but he said, 'Tell David about the coyotes. He'll know what to do.' I think he was out of his head." She shrugged. "It didn't seem important at the time, what with you being taken down in the same cave-in. I couldn't be bothering you about wild beasts with you hurt in bed at the time."

David rubbed his palms down his cheeks. "Were you having trouble with coyotes in the mining camp?"

" We had some trouble a while back with a pack digging through the rubbish heap and killing some chickens, but Paddy took his rifle and cleared them out."

"Has anyone else reported trouble?"

"Nay. Paddy said to tell you and no other. The poor man was agitated about it, mixing things up in his mind. No doubt he was thinking back to the bit o' trouble with the pesky creatures and worried they might return. I don't know why he wanted me to tell you, but he did, and I have." She levered her hands on her knees and rose. "Me duty's done with the telling. I'll be heading to the rooming house. It's getting terrible late, and me train leaves at seven."

Karen walked the older woman to the door. "You're sure you don't need anything? You have enough money?"

"'Tis a good lady you are, Mrs. Mackenzie. I have more than enough. Your husband's family has seen to that. I've plenty to get home on. I'll be praying for you and the mister. Such a sorrow about his eyes, and him such a fine gentleman."

"Thank you. You will be careful getting to your rooming house, won't you?"

Buckford cleared his throat behind them. "Perhaps I could escort your guest to her rooming house?"

"That's very thoughtful of you. Thank you."

Karen closed the door behind them. Had the visit done more harm than good? Mrs. Doolin's words made no sense, and yet, Paddy Doolin had used practically his dying breath to implore her to get his message to David. What could varmints possibly have to do with the accident? Nothing, that's what. As she said, the man was out of his head.

A pile of letters on the hall table caught her eye. She sorted through them, bills and accounts, the newspaper, circulars, and personal correspondence. Perhaps David would like her to read the newspaper to him before bedtime.

Aunt Hattie would be scandalized if she knew Karen read the newspaper. Speaking of Aunt Hattie, a fat letter from her lay at the bottom of the stack. Karen scooped up the paper and the letter and returned to the parlor.

David sat before the fireplace, his face in his hands. When

she took the chair across from him, he sat up and sighed. "She's gone then?"

"Yes, Buckford is seeing her to the rooming house. Did you know her husband well?"

"Paddy Doolin was the best dynamiter in Martin City. Every mining engineer in the Rockies tried to pinch him from us. A giant of a man and as capable as they come, always smiling and laughing. I can't think why he'd want to tell me about a problem he'd taken care of himself."

"More likely he wasn't in his right senses."

David thought on this. "That could explain it. Or maybe she misunderstood." He smacked his thigh with his fist. "I thought maybe she had a clue for me, something that Paddy knew that would tell me why the shaft collapsed—Something to tell me what I did wrong."

"Isn't it possible that it isn't anyone's fault?"

He shook his head. "Something caused that cave-in. Marcus is supposed to be looking into it, but I haven't heard anything from him." His feet shifted, and he pounded his leg again. "Though if he finds something that shows I was at fault, I don't know if he would tell me."

She needed to change the subject, give David something else to think about before bedtime. "I sorted the mail." She tugged at her bottom lip. "The evening paper arrived while we were out. Would you like me to read to you?"

"No, thank you."

She swallowed her disappointment. "There's a letter from Aunt Hattie, too." Slipping a hairpin from her coiled hair, Karen slit the envelope and withdrew the closely written pages. She tilted the paper toward the fireplace and scanned the first page. A wave of homesickness sloshed over her, and a lump formed in her throat.

"David, she's invited us for Christmas." A smile stretched her lips. "Wouldn't that be wonderful? I miss her so much.

When she got sick, I was so afraid. She's the only one I have left from my family. I don't know what I'd do without her." She turned the page. "Listen to this:

> *You and David could make a visit here part of your honeymoon trip. We could spend the holidays together. It would be like old times to have you with me. I get so lonely for you at Christmas. I remember how you love everything about this time of year. Even if you could only come for a week or two, it would make me so happy. I'd travel to see you, but the doctor is advising against it at the moment, the old fusspot. I think he's planning to send his children to college on the fees he collects from me. Anyway, do say you'll come."*

Karen lowered the letter. "David, Christmas in Kansas City, won't that be fun? I'm not sure where the time has gotten to. It's only two weeks until the twenty-fifth. I'll have to do some shopping and see about tickets."

"Karen, stop."

"But there's so much to see to. I should start making a list, so I don't forget anything." She bounded out of the chair and headed for the desk to find a pencil. What a blessing it would be to talk face-to-face with her aunt. Christmas with family. Her eyes grew misty at the thought.

"Karen."

His voice was so sharp, she stopped with the drawer only half open. "What?"

"I'm not going to Kansas City."

Her mouth fell open. "But. . ." She blinked, her heart tumbling into her shoes. "It's Aunt Hattie."

"I'm not going to Kansas City for Christmas. I'm not going to Martin City for Christmas. I'm not going anywhere for Christmas."

"But you went out tonight and everything went fine." Except for the way their kiss ended. She touched her lips, remembering the bliss of being in his arms. "And Aunt Hattie won't judge or make you uncomfortable. You've never met a kinder soul. She'll love you. I wanted you to meet her at the wedding." Her voice hitched. "The doctor told her she'd be well enough to travel by early summer when we originally planned to marry. Since we moved up the wedding date and she wasn't able to come, this will be the perfect solution. It shouldn't interrupt your studies too much. We'll be back in less than a month. Two weeks if that is all you can spare."

"You're not listening to me." His hands fisted and relaxed, only to fist again. "I am not traveling. There's a big difference between a few hours' visit to the school and traipsing across the plains to stay in the house of a complete stranger."

"But she's not a stranger. She's family."

"No, Karen. This is not open for discussion."

Karen took in his impassive face, as stubborn and set as ever, and clenched her teeth. Tears gathered in her eyes and spilled over. One fat drop plopped onto Aunt Hattie's invitation. Karen folded the pages and stuffed them into the envelope to read later. "Very well." She couldn't keep the sound of tears out of her voice and didn't care. She wanted him to know how much he'd hurt her. Why must she be the one to always sacrifice? "I'm going to bed." Before she gave vent to the harsh words she wanted to hurl at him, she escaped.

❧

David pushed his forehead against the heels of his hands. He'd made her cry. Again. But couldn't she see she asked more than he could give? A train trip? To a strange city, to a strange house? To be presented to her sole remaining family member as the cripple she'd married?

No. He couldn't do it. They would spend the holidays here. But maybe he could make it up to her—extend the peace of the season and make some smaller concessions. He'd grown weary of his own recalcitrance. Perhaps it was possible for them to achieve some measure of happiness together. Tomorrow he'd talk to Buckford about sending a message home. Karen's Christmas gift lay in his bureau drawer at the house. Mother could send it in plenty of time.

Straightening, he leaned back in the chair and rested his head, pushing his guilt over Karen to the back of his mind. For now, he would examine everything Mrs. Doolin had said about her husband's last words. Perhaps, if he thought on it enough, he could make some sense of the cryptic message.

twelve

The letter to Aunt Hattie needed two stamps, but it weighed much less than Karen's spirit. She battled down resentment and tried to understand things from David's perspective, but it took much prayer and soul-searching, and nothing she did seemed to alleviate the heaviness. In the same mail, she sent a letter to David's parents, declining both their invitation for Karen and David to come to Martin City and their offer to journey to Denver so they could all be together for the holidays. She shopped for gifts and contemplated the idea of going by herself, but the thought of spending their first married Christmas apart didn't sit well with her, and she discarded the idea. Perhaps he'd feel more confident by springtime and they could travel to see Aunt Hattie together. Or Hattie could come to them as soon as the doctor gave her leave.

The closer they drew to Christmas Day, the more homesick and lonely Karen became. The package from Aunt Hattie nearly broke her heart. Buckford brought her the crate and helped her open it. Beneath layers of excelsior, she unearthed the hand-carved crèche and figures of her aunt's beloved nativity set. Brought from Europe by Karen's great-grandmother, it had held a place of honor in the Worth household. The card expressed Hattie's disappointment at not being together for the holidays, but now that Karen had her own home, the nativity should be hers. Karen didn't try to stop the tears as she lifted the wooden animals and shepherds and wise men from the crate and set them on the mantel. Each dear, loved figurine only made her miss her aunt more. By the time she lifted the natal family into place, she was sobbing.

Voices in the hall had her scrambling to mop the tears and present at least a facade of calm. Lessons must be over for the day. She straightened her hair and tucked her handkerchief away and went to say good-bye to Rex until the new year. When she reached the doorway, she stopped, not wanting to interrupt.

"You'll never have any measure of independence until you're willing to leave the safety of this house. Why won't you even take a walk down the street with me? You have to be weary of being cooped up here day after day. The only place you've gone in almost two months is a single reception at the school, and I had to strong-arm you into going then." Rex placed his hat on his head and his hand on the doorknob. His walking stick, twin to one he'd brought for David that stood unused in the umbrella stand, jutted from under his arm. "Your training won't be complete until you can go where you want, when you want."

"I don't need that. I wish you'd stop pushing me."

"It's my job to push you."

"Then it's my job to push back. I appreciate what you've done for me—teaching me to read again, to eat and dress and organize. I don't want anything beyond that."

"But there's so much more that you're capable of. So much more you could do."

"Good-bye, Rex. Until the new year."

Rex left unsatisfied, and Karen sympathized with him. She was unsatisfied, too.

❧

Early on Christmas morning, Karen donned a russet wool dress and wrapped her cape about her shoulders. As she passed David's door, she had to blink back tears. In spite of her best efforts, she had gotten no further than Rex had, and David refused to accompany her to church, not even on Christmas.

Though he must have felt some remorse for denying her

request that they go to her aunt's. Or maybe it was the holiday that brought about the subtle changes. He had seemed softer these past few days.

She slipped into the back pew and surveyed the congregation. How she missed the fellowship of the little whitewashed church in Martin City and dear old Pastor Van Dyke's sermons. Though the soaring spaces and stained glass of this large church in Denver inspired awe and she was surrounded by many times the number of worshippers in Martin City, the experience left her remote and cold. The droning, vibrating tones from the pipe organ sent chills across her flesh, and she shivered as she opened her Bible for the reading.

If she and David had gone to Kansas City for Christmas, she would be sitting with Aunt Hattie in the nice church Karen had visited when she went there to take care of her aunt. Was it really less than three months since she'd been there, listening to the young preacher, Silas Hamilton, deliver a poignant and stirring message? If she was with Hattie in that church, Christmas and Christ would seem very near.

As it was, she sat through the formal service, detached and unable to focus. Her thoughts bounced from missing her aunt, who was distant from her by days and miles, to frustration with her husband, who was distant from her by pride and fear.

When she got home, she draped her cloak over the banister to carry to her room later and wandered into the parlor. Off-key humming accompanied the clank of cookware from the back of the house and made her smile. Taking a long match from the holder on the wall, she touched it to the coal fire then went around the room lighting the candles among the pine and holly. Not even the spicy, resinous scents that mingled with the smell of roasting goose lifted her spirits.

"God Rest Ye, Merry Gentlemen" boomed from the kitchen. Mrs. Webber, a choir of one.

Karen stopped before the nativity scene, touching the pieces lightly, her heart sending Christmas wishes to her aunt and to David's family. Karen fingered the cameo at her throat, a gift from the Mackenzies.

She turned when footsteps sounded in the hall. "Hello, David. Merry Christmas." She forced the words out. So far the day had been anything but merry.

"You're back. How was church?" He crossed the room easily and reached for his chair.

"Fine. It's a beautiful building, lots of brick and stained glass. Their organist is very. . .enthusiastic."

The corner of his mouth quirked. "So is Mrs. Webber. She's been singing carols all morning. I think it's her not-so-subtle way of bringing Christmas cheer into the house." He breathed deeply. "Though I have to admit, the place sure smells like Christmas. Would you like your gift now?"

Her head came up. "I didn't know if we would be exchanging gifts. I got you something, too." Weeks ago.

"I know you've been upset with me about staying here alone for the holidays, and I'm sorry you were disappointed. Maybe we can declare a truce from hurt feelings for today?" He spread his hands, palms up. "After all, it is Christmas."

She tugged on her lower lip then dropped her hand to her lap with a sigh. "Very well. You're right." A wry smile touched her lips. "Peace on earth, goodwill toward men."

"That's the spirit." He pulled open his jacket and dug into the inner pocket. "Now I can return your greeting. Merry Christmas, Karen." He withdrew a velvet pouch and held it out to her. When she hesitated, he swung it toward her a bit. "Go on. It's for you."

She took the bag and loosened the drawstring. Running her fingers over the gold-embossed jeweler's name on the bottom of the pouch, she tipped it upside down. A glittering ribbon of white and red stones slid into her hand. She gasped then breathed, "David."

He smiled. "I bought that when I bought your engagement ring. The garnets match the setting in your ring. Do you like it?"

The jewels captured and shot back the lights from the candles, winking warmly as she turned them. "They're beautiful." She rose and went to the mirror over the mantel where she draped the necklace at her throat. "Thank you." A lump formed in her throat.

He came to stand behind her. She stood stock-still when he cupped her shoulders. "Their beauty must pale beside your own. You always were the most beautiful woman in any company." Then, as if he thought he had gone too far, he stepped back and shoved his hands into his pockets. "Now, what's this about a gift you have for me?"

Karen turned from the mirror and laid the necklace on the table beside her chair. "It's in my room. I'll get it." A truce, for today. Their marriage so far had been one long, pitched battle interrupted by small truces. When would they reach an accord they could both be happy with? She retrieved the package from her bottom bureau drawer and returned to the parlor.

David stood at the mantel, his fingers trailing over the nativity figurines. When she entered, he turned toward her. "That's a really fine set. The carving seems so detailed, and there are so many pieces. It was nice of your aunt to gift it to you."

She exhaled slowly. "I think it would be in the best interest of our truce if we don't talk about Aunt Hattie. Please, sit down and I'll hand you your present."

When he had resumed his seat, she placed the squareish object into his hands and stepped back. The qualms she had when she first bought it came galloping back. Would he think the present emphasized his blindness? Or would he realize she only wanted to help him? She laced her fingers under her chin and waited.

Slowly, he pulled the end of the store twine and pushed back the brown paper. His fingertips grazed the fine wood.

"An abacus." The beads whispered on the rods and clacked together when he tilted the frame.

"I found it in a shop downtown. The owner is Chinese, and the place was stuffed with herbs and tea and artwork. I saw this in the window, and it was so pretty, much better than the one Rex loaned you from the school." She knelt beside his chair and spun one of the wooden beads. "The frame is cherry, the rods white hard maple, and the beads are polished walnut." She searched his face for a reaction. "I thought it might be useful."

He flattened his palm and ran it across the face of the abacus, rotating the walnut disks. "This is really fine. Thank you."

"You like it? It's all right?"

"Very much. You're very thoughtful." He reached out and touched her hair, letting his fingers trail down her cheek. Then his hand dropped away. "How about if we go in search of our Christmas dinner. It must be nearly time to eat."

"You're eating with me?" She tipped back on her heels and gripped the arm of his chair to steady herself.

He rose and the paper and string in his lap drifted to the floor. "Would you mind?"

She gathered the paper and tossed it on the fire, trying not to read too much into his offer. "I'd like that." Smiling for the first time in days, she tucked her hand into his arm.

He set the abacus on the table beside his chair and walked with her to the back of the house.

❧

Late that night, David sat in his bedroom with the abacus in his lap. Idly, his fingers did calculations while his mind drifted. Dinner together had been a success from where he sat. He'd managed not to spill anything on himself or her, and the conversation had flowed passably well.

In keeping with both their families' traditions, once they'd returned to the parlor, Karen had read aloud the Christmas story from Luke chapter two. They'd passed the rest of the evening with Karen reading aloud from a new book Sam had given her for Christmas, *Life on the Mississippi* by Mark Twain. David had relaxed in his chair and let her voice take him through a history of the mighty river and Twain's exploits as a riverboat pilot. Altogether the best evening they'd spent together in months.

He ran his hand along the abacus frame. A beautiful and thoughtful gift. Useful, too. He wished he'd known how to use one before the cave-in. It would've lessened his workload considerably not having to work everything out on paper.

His mind turned back to his work. The images of his maps and drawings remained firm in his head, the calculations and projections. He still hadn't been able to find the weakness. Where had he gone wrong? If he was starting from scratch on the project, what would he change? And where did Paddy Doolin's message come in? Was it just the raving of a dying man or did it have some bearing on the cave-in?

David rubbed his forehead and got up to prepare for bed. The more he worried the problem like a terrier with a rat, the more muddled he became. Perhaps he'd have to accept the fact that he would never know where he'd gone wrong. Marcus had remained silent, which meant either he hadn't found anything or he'd found something he didn't think David should know. Relief mingled with defeat as he thought about letting go of the past.

He set the abacus on the desk in the corner. A smile pulled at the corner of his mouth. He wished he could've seen Karen's face to determine if she really liked the necklace and if she recognized it for what it was: a peace offering. Just like the cave-in, perhaps it was time he accepted things the way they were and get on with living, an action that included letting go of his fears and having a normal marriage—or as normal as he could manage—with his beautiful wife.

Worms of doubt wriggled through him, whispering that he was a fool to consider it, that he wasn't man enough, that he would only get his heart broken.

Stop it. You tried to hold Karen at arm's length, but it didn't work, did it? She's in your heart, and you need her. Not having Karen in your life would be worse than being blind. You should be doing everything in your power to make her happy. You heard it in her voice when you did something as simple as eating dinner with her tonight.

One successful dinner didn't mean he was ready to conquer the world, but perhaps it wasn't too early to begin planning a trip to Kansas City in the spring. He wouldn't tell Karen right away, but when Rex came back after the first of the year, David would take him up on his offer to learn to navigate the streets of Denver by himself.

thirteen

Karen looked up from her correspondence when Buckford entered the room. "Ah, thank you for the interruption. I think my writing hand is about to fall off. I could use a cup of tea."

"A telegram arrived for you, ma'am." He held out an envelope. "I'll see to your tea right away."

"Thank you. Would you see if David would like some tea or coffee? I think he's still upstairs reading."

Buckford nodded and left.

Karen leaned back in her chair and rubbed her wrist. She'd long grown weary of sending out her regrets for one party after another. She hadn't known the Mackenzies knew so many people in Denver, nor that their friends were so social. Each invitation to a ball, soiree, or fete must be answered, and the deluge of envelopes for tonight's New Year's Eve festivities had taken most of the morning to respond to. A yawn tugged at her jaw, and she turned her attention to the telegram.

Mrs. David Mackenzie
    Regret to inform you Miss H. Worth passed away last evening, Dec. 30. Funeral scheduled Jan. 4. Church sends condolences and lawyer awaits instructions.

                                                    Rev. S. Hamilton.

Karen read the words, each one slicing like jagged glass. Tears blurred the type, and the paper fell from her nerveless fingers. A deep trembling started in her middle and radiated outward, chilling as it went. A fist of pain lodged in her throat.

Sobbing reached her ears, a mournful cry torn from an anguished soul. She tried to shut it out until she realized it came from her. Loss crept around her like a black mist, and the room began to whirl.

Buckford rattled the teacups when he plonked the tray down and hurried to her side.

Karen put out her hand to grip the edge of the desk.

"Ma'am? Are you all right? Should I call someone?" In an unprecedented move, he took her arm. "Perhaps you'll feel better if you lie on the couch." He didn't wait for her assent but helped her to her feet and put his arm around her waist, assisting her to the settee.

A small, detached part of her mind reasoned that she must look very shocked and shaky indeed for Buckford to break protocol like this. She lay back against the cushions and stared at the ceiling.

Tears leaked from the corners of her eyes, wetting her temples and trailing into her ears, but she didn't care. Aunt Hattie was dead. Her heart throbbed as if a giant heel had ground on it. She would never see her beloved aunt again on this earth.

"Lie still. I'll get some help." Buckford patted her shoulder then disappeared into the foyer.

Karen couldn't have moved if she wanted to. Boulders of grief tumbled over her, swallowing her in an avalanche.

Footsteps clattered on the stairs, and David knelt beside her. "What is it, Karen? Are you ill?" He felt over her arms and legs. Then his fingers touched her tear-soaked face. "Are you hurt?"

His caress burned her skin. Anger such as she'd never felt before welled up inside her, and energy returned like a lightning flash. She shoved his hands away. "Don't touch me." Grabbing the back of the settee, she struggled upright, banging into David in the process.

He rocked and tumbled onto his backside. "Karen, what's the matter with you?" He leaned back on his palms, his eyebrows climbing toward his hairline.

She got up and brushed past him toward the desk. The telegram lay on the floor by the chair, and when she reached down for it, the blood rushed to her head, renewing her dizziness. She snatched up the paper and crumpled it to her chest. Her control cracked, and she spewed out hurt-laden words. "My aunt passed away last night, and thanks to you and your colossal selfishness, I wasn't there." A spike-laden sob clawed its way out of her throat, choking her.

David clambered to his feet and approached her with his hand outstretched.

She shrank from him, pushing into the corner. If he touched her, she would be sick. "Stay away from me."

His hand dropped to his side. "Karen, I'm so sorry about your aunt."

She shook her head. Tears dripped from her chin onto the telegram. "No, you're not. You didn't even know her. You didn't want to visit her. She was the only person I had who really loved me. And now she's gone."

"That's not true. Karen, I love you. Let me help you through this." He reached for her again, but she evaded his grasp.

"You don't love me. I thought you did once, but I was wrong. If you loved me, you would've married me without being coerced. You would've let me help you, and you would've treated me like your bride. I'm a secretary not a wife, taking care of household accounts, overseeing the help, writing your correspondence. No matter what I do, you still aren't ready to love me more than you love yourself. You keep me at a distance. You never share your thoughts and feelings unless you're angry or bitter, and then you deny me the chance to see Aunt Hattie one last time. Does that sound like love to you?" She choked on a sob and pressed her knuckles to her mouth, not wanting to look at him anymore. She only wanted to get out of the room, to find somewhere she could breathe and think and grieve. Knocking his outstretched hand away, Karen hurried to escape.

"Where are you going?"

She paused at the doorway. "I'm going to pack. I have a funeral to attend." She brushed past Buckford at the bottom of the stairs. "And don't even think about offering to come with me. It's too late for that."

❧

Her door slammed at the top of the stairs as effectively as she'd slammed the door on his efforts to comfort her.

David groped for the edge of the settee and sank onto it. He put his face into his hands, trying to make sense of what had just happened, but only one thing stood out in his mind.

She was leaving him.

Packing her bags and boarding a train.

The truth hit like a blow from an ax handle. Though he had tried to prepare himself for it from the moment he married her, the reality halved his heart. He had let his guard down, had actually started imagining she might stay with him, that together they could find happiness in spite of his infirmity. What if he had gone with her to her aunt's? Would she have come back to him if he had sent her alone?

She thinks I don't love her.

Shoving his fingers into his hair, he squeezed his hands into fists. Her accusations zipped through his head, and he was guilty of every one of them. He *had* held her away from him and kept his most intimate and personal thoughts to himself. Because he had been afraid and ashamed, he had refused to accompany her on a family visit. But that didn't mean he didn't love her.

He had been trying for days now to think of a way to swallow his pride and tell her he wanted to be a real husband to her, to share their lives together the way they had planned when he first asked her to marry him. He'd even had Buckford send a note to Rex about learning to get around outside the house starting as soon as the winter break ended in order to be ready to take Karen on a trip in the spring.

But it was too late now. She was leaving him. She didn't want him to go with her, and he had no right to ask her to stay.

He pushed himself up from the settee and shuffled across the room to the doorway. "Buckford?"

David jumped when a voice came from quite close by. "Yes?"

"My wife"—the words jabbed—"is going on a trip. I would appreciate it if you would go to the depot and procure her ticket in a private compartment with a sleeper. Spare no expense. I want the best you can get. Then go find a shop and procure a traveling blanket and pillow and some reading matter. Anything you can think of to make the trip easier." He swallowed against the ache growing in his middle. "When you get back, be ready to take her to the station."

"Very good, sir." Buckford's voice held not a note of censure. "One ticket?"

"One ticket, Buckford. There's money in the cash box upstairs." He hadn't been in the office since they'd moved into the town house. He'd shut the door on that part of his life. After handing Buckford the key to the cash box, David resumed his seat in the study, helpless to do anything else.

What seemed like hours later, Buckford returned to the town house. The smell of smoke and sunshine lingered on his clothes. "Sir, I've been to the depot." He pressed a pasteboard rectangle into David's hand. "Here is the ticket. I did as you asked and reserved a private compartment in a Pullman car. The train leaves in two hours." He paused. "There is still room on the train if you should choose to accompany her. I can pack for you very quickly."

David shook his head. "No, she has enough details to see to

without having to look out for me, too. Though I'd like to be there to support her during the funeral, she'll have an easier time without me." Just as he'd thought. Life would be easier for her without his clogging things up and needing to be looked after. "Check with her to see if she needs any telegrams sent ahead to anyone and be sure to cable the depot in Kansas City and have a carriage waiting for her and someone to handle the baggage."

"Very well."

Before Buckford could leave, David rose and touched his arm. "Thank you, Buckford, for taking care of all these details I can't do myself."

"My pleasure, sir."

A giant fist crushed David's chest. Mackenzie history was repeating itself, and he was helpless to stop it.

He accompanied her to the depot. She didn't speak to him on the journey, and she didn't cry.

He recalled the last time he had seen Karen before the accident, the last time he'd put her on a train. Bags at her feet, checking her pocketbook for her ticket, torn with excitement at seeing her aunt again, worried about Hattie's ill health, and saddened to be parted from him, even for a little while. She had chattered all the way to the train that day. He hadn't been conflicted in the least. He had known without a doubt he would miss her every day they were apart, and his world wouldn't be right until she returned. With no regard for the fact that they were standing on the platform at the depot with anyone and everyone looking on, he had swept her into his arms and kissed her. His embrace had knocked her hat askew, but she hadn't seemed to mind, returning his kiss with passion. He had looked into her beautiful blue eyes and brushed her lips with his once more before putting her on the train.

This time, he might've been a stranger to her. She took the ticket he presented her while Buckford instructed a porter to label her trunk and wheel it to the baggage car.

David stood helplessly by, listening to the sounds the train made, hissing and clicking in preparation for its trip across the plains. "You've got money for your meals and anything you might need?"

"Yes, David."

"You'll cable when you arrive?"

"Yes."

"If you need more money, the First Union Bank in Kansas City will honor your personal check. Or I can wire you funds."

"Yes."

The train whistle shattered the air, startling him. Someone—the conductor?—shouted, "All aboard!"

All he wanted to say jammed in his throat. He settled for touching her arm, her shoulder, then her face before lowering his lips to her cool cheek. "Good-bye, Karen."

She moved away, and Buckford guided him back from the train. With a growl, tons of metal began to move. Steamy mist drifted across his skin and the smell of cinders and ash filled the air.

fourteen

January 4, 1884

Dear Karen,

Buckford is writing this for me, as my own handwriting is still deplorable, and in any case, I don't like using the metal frame to write for myself.

Thank you for sending the wire confirming your safe arrival. Buckford tells me the funeral is today, and I hope you will accept my condolences.

Things are much the same here. Rex is coming to resume our lessons on Monday.

I am sure you are busy settling your aunt's estate, so I won't take any more of your time. It's awkward dictating to Buckford. I never realized before how easy it was to speak my mind when it was you taking down my correspondence. I guess we never realize what we have until it is gone.

Do you know when you will be coming home?

Sincerely,
David

Karen spread the page out on her black skirt and read the scant lines for the tenth time. How different from the love letters he had mailed to her the last time she stayed in this house. Though with all that had happened to them and between them, it wasn't surprising.

We never realize what we have until it is gone.

How many times had that truth been brought home to her over the past week? She glanced at the calendar on

Aunt Hattie's kitchen wall. Monday, the seventh. Rex would be there now. Would he be making David use the despised handwriting frame and practice his letters?

The funeral had been the loneliest day of her life. Her heart ached for Aunt Hattie, and every time Karen turned around, she expected to see her aunt's dear face. Pastor Hamilton delivered a beautiful service, touching and full of remembrances and words of comfort. Later, Karen knew she would draw on those words, once she could think about them without breaking down. She withdrew a black handkerchief from her sleeve and dabbed her eyes before folding David's letter and putting it back in the envelope.

David.

Under the layers of grief for her aunt, Karen had piled up a store of guilt for the way she'd treated her husband, for the harsh words she'd spewed at him. That guilt was in no way assuaged by the knowledge that she had been in shock, overwhelmed with loss and sorrow.

Tiredness washed over her, a lethargy that had dogged her on the endless train trip and continued through the funeral. Her thoughts were wooly and chased each other like fat, stumbling sheep. She didn't know which one to follow, so she followed none. For now, Aunt Hattie's house was a safe, soothing refuge where she didn't have to think too much and didn't have to battle her stubborn husband. She could just drift.

Pushing back the teacup, she rose and went to the bedroom to lie down. She'd think about her husband later.

୬

February 1, 1884

Dear David,
  Thank you for your note of January 4. I apologize that it has taken me so long to send a letter in return. I've been

so tired and absorbed with a thousand details. Settling an estate, even one in such good order as my aunt's, takes time. I've been going through her things, trying to decide what to keep and what to give away. Everything holds memories for me. The sorting is going slowly.

Pastor Hamilton has been very good, stopping by to visit at least once a week with some of the ladies from the church. The church here reminds me of the congregation in Martin City. Many of Hattie's friends have come by as well, and they have welcomed me into their church family. It feels good to be a part of their congregation, to be accepted and cared for. I've never really felt at home in the church in Denver, though that is probably because I always attended alone.

Hattie's friends are a delight and have banded together in a matchmaking scheme that occupies them constantly. Pastor Hamilton is a handsome, single man, and they would like nothing more than to see him properly and happily wed. He is, however, quite adept at outmaneuvering them. I am surprised at his dexterity in avoiding their traps.

The lawyer seeing to probating Aunt Hattie's will, a Mr. Drury, is currently unavailable. He's gone to Springfield on family business. It appears his daughter has made an unadvisable match, and he's gone to see about helping her obtain an annulment. I hope he is successful in extricating her from this trouble. He seems a dear man, and he's very upset about the situation, as I'm sure you can understand.

As to your question about when I will return, I'm afraid I don't have an answer. Things have been so strained between us. Perhaps this time apart will benefit us both. You can concentrate on nothing but your work with Rex, and I can think things through. In any case, there is still much to be done here, and I cannot come home until it is completed.

Sincerely,
Karen

"Read it again, Buckford." David folded his hands in his lap then remembered to add, "Please."

The houseman read the letter once more, slowly. "Would you like to dictate a reply, sir?"

He stirred. "Later." At the moment, he could think of no way to frame a reply that wouldn't either sound dictatorial or pleading. "Could I have the letter, please?" He took the paper and tucked it into his jacket over his heart. "That will be all, Buckford. Thank you."

When the houseman's footsteps receded, David was left with nothing but his thoughts chasing one another like ravenous wolves. His insides writhed as he lined up the facts. A month had passed before she could bother to send a letter. The handsome, single pastor was coming to call, and the ladies of the church were matchmaking. Karen mentioned an annulment case, and she didn't know when she would be coming home. Even a blind man could put those pieces together. All the excitement surging through him when Buckford brought a letter from her had dried to a trickle of guilt-ridden malaise for having driven her to these circumstances.

Would she come home at all? Had he lost her for good? Was this how Uncle Frank had felt, as if everything truly precious in his life was slipping away and there was nothing he could do to change it?

❧

February 11, 1884

Dear Karen,
 As you can see, i'm writing this letter myself, and of necessity will be brief. the situation being what it is, please take all the time you need. i am fine here. buckford is taking very good care of me. and mrs. webber too.

David

Karen stared at the letter, a total of a quarter of a page, and her heart wept. Not because he had written it himself, though that fact was poignant enough, but because of his words.

Take all the time you need. I am fine.

What had she expected? A stern, laying-down-of-the-law order to wrap things up here quickly and get herself home? What had she hoped for? Declarations of love and longing and a plea for her to return to him as soon as she could? The paper blurred.

She had gotten neither. He didn't need her, and he didn't want her back. He couldn't have put it more plainly. Buckford and Mrs. Webber were seeing to all his needs, and she was to take her sweet time.

Her throat closed, and she put her head down on her arms on the kitchen table.

❧

March 31, 1884

Dear David,

I have finally completed the task of winding up Aunt Hattie's estate. The house has been sold and the new occupants will take up residence tomorrow. The possessions dearest to my heart have been crated and will reside in storage under the care of Mr. Drury until I can direct him to the best place to forward them. Those items I did not wish to keep I have sold and donated the proceeds to the church here.

I will miss this church family. They have included me in every way and made my stay here so much easier than it could have been. I'm sorry to be leaving them, though I know I will see them all again someday.

I received another letter from your mother this week. She tells me that Pastor Van Dyke is ready to retire and that the denomination has sent them the name of his successor. Imagine my happy surprise to know that the man who will take up the pastorate in Martin City is none other than Silas Hamilton, who has been such a good friend to me here. He has often mentioned his desire to move farther west, and he is eager, after hearing my stories of the beauties of life in the Rocky Mountains, to relocate to Martin City. He expects to preach his first sermon there by Independence Day at the latest. I am sure the parishioners, including your parents, will make him most welcome.

As I had hoped when I left Denver three months ago, this time apart has given me room to consider our marriage, the unorthodox way it came about, the barely civil way it has been conducted, and where it should go from here. I am hopeful that we can discuss our future rationally and without recriminations. It should be obvious to both of us that we cannot continue this way. I know we can sort things out to both our satisfactions if we just try. To that end, as soon as I turn the house keys over to the new occupants, I will board a train for Denver. I expect to arrive early on the morning of April 4.

Sincerely,
Karen

"She'll arrive the day after tomorrow." David tilted his abacus slowly forward and back, listening to the slide and click of the beads. Would she stay? For how long? Would she come seeking an annulment? Would she listen if he tried to apologize?

Buckford slid the letter across the desktop. "It will be very nice for the church in Martin City to have a new pastor so quickly."

With a stab, David remembered that Buckford was a member of the church in Martin City. Uprooting and moving to Denver to get away from his family and the scene of his accident had caused turmoil in not only his life and Karen's but Buckford's as well.

The front bell shrilled, and a fist pounded on the door. Buckford's hasty steps on the hardwood weren't in time to open the door before it crashed wide. "Dave, where are you?"

"Sam? What are you doing here?" David pushed himself up from his chair and braced himself for Sam's familiar crushing handshake and hearty backslap.

"I figured you'd stewed down here in Denver long enough. You've ignored all my letters." Cloth moved and damp air swirled. "Thank you, Buckford. I needed that coat when I left home, but it looks like spring has come around here. Oh, and I left my bag and a box on the front stoop. Could you slide them inside for me?"

David resumed his seat. Sam sagged into the chair opposite, and David could feel his brother's appraisal on his skin.

"We need to talk." Sam's boots scraped on the floor and the springs in his chair creaked.

"What about?" David tensed.

"Quite a few things, actually, but a couple items are vying for the top of the list. We need to talk about the mine, and after that, we need to talk about Karen."

"I have no desire to talk about the mine, and Karen is none of your business." The familiar shell of defensiveness, the walls he'd been working so hard to lower, flew up again, full strength. He took a grip on himself and battled down the old feelings.

The sigh Sam emitted seemed to come from his toes. "Dave, I don't want to fight with you. I strongly disagree that Karen is none of my business since she's my sister-in-law and I care about her. I'll leave off talking about her for now, but we have to talk about the mine. I need help, and you're the only one I trust. I can't go to anyone else with this. Not yet."

The earnest edge to Sam's voice sent uneasiness skittering across David's skin. He sat forward and put his elbows on his knees. "What's wrong at the mine, and why can't you talk about it to anyone else?"

"When Mother sent Buckford to you before Christmas, I gave him a box of papers and samples. Where is that?"

"I'm not sure. I think it's in my office upstairs. My papers have been the last thing on my mind in recent months."

"Well, you'd best stoke up that brain of yours for some hard slog. I'll ask Buckford to bring some sandwiches and coffee to the office. What I have to say is going to take a while."

fifteen

David took the chair behind the desk in his office upstairs and placed his hands on the carved, wooden arms.

Sam entered and something weighty hit the desktop. "Now, where's that other box? Ah, here it is." Papers rustled, and David recognized the clack and grit of rocks scraping against each other. "Let me move this inkwell and spread out some of these pages." Thumps and bumps as Sam got things settled.

David couldn't ignore the dueling excitement and fear in his middle. Excitement at delving, even in a small way, into his former occupation and fear that he wouldn't be up to the task. What if Sam had come all this way, putting his faith in his older brother, and David let him down? David couldn't help but feel he faced a test tonight, one he desperately wanted to pass.

"What are you looking for, and what help do you think I can give?"

Sam dragged a chair close. "First, you can tell me I'm not going crazy or missing something and jumping to the wrong conclusion. Then I want to compare some of the paperwork I sent with Buckford with what I brought today. Something isn't right, and I have a feeling it hasn't been right for longer than any of us would like to think."

Buckford arrived with a tray, and the aroma of hot coffee filled the room. Matches scritched and glass tinked as he moved around the room lighting the wall sconces.

David sipped his coffee while Sam rummaged through the boxes again.

"Buckford, why don't you stay?" Sam asked. "You know a lot more than you ever let on, and you've been in the mines. You might see something I missed. What's that contraption?"

Bumpy wood touched David's hand. "I thought you could use this, sir."

David closed his fingers on his abacus. "Thank you, Buckford. Sam's right. Stay and listen. Sam, stop fidgeting with that stuff and cut through the chaff."

Sam sighed and stilled. "All right. At first, I thought the trouble at the mine started with the cave-in, but looking back on things, I can see indications that something was going on even before then."

David's chin came up. "What?"

"Well, think about it, Dave. Remember that axle on the ore wagon that broke? The team had to be shot, broken legs on both. Then there was all the trouble at the company store. First, somebody makes a big error on ordering and supplies run short. Then, the day after the new inventory comes in, the store is robbed and ransacked. We thought these were just coincidences, but what if they weren't?"

"That's reaching a bit, Sam. There were a few petty thefts in town around the time the store was robbed, and wagon axles have been known to break before."

"True, but what about the four braces of mules that were stolen? Then we get a bad batch of blasting caps. And in September, I spent nearly the whole month working on one pump or another. Parts that shouldn't have failed did. Fluids 'accidentally' drained away. Debris 'somehow' got into the motor. I couldn't keep more than two pumps going at a time, and we were running in circles to keep the mine dry. Then there was the cave-in."

"That was my fault." David's shoulders slumped, and he rubbed his temple.

Sam gripped David's shoulder. "I know you think that, but

why? You've never come up with a definitive reason why the supports should have failed and neither has anyone else. I think we need to comb through all the paperwork again—the plans, the surveys, and the ore samples—and figure this out."

"How can I? I can't see." David straightened and gripped the arms of his chair. The familiar helplessness rolled over him.

"I'll help you. I think the answer is here, but I can't find it on my own. Last week, the mine office was ransacked twice. I think whoever it was that did it was looking for the papers that have been in your house the past few months. Nothing else was missing. Marcus and I checked."

David frowned. "Why didn't you have Marcus look these things over? He's the better engineer. If he'd been in charge of the mine, the cave-in wouldn't have happened."

Sam rose and paced the area in front of the desk. "Dave, I'll match my time on a rock drill or pickax against any man in the mine. I can about sharpen a pencil with a stick of dynamite, but I can't decipher these charts and papers by myself. I need you. Not Marcus, not Father, you. I'll read aloud anything you want me to. I'll help you do the figures, but I know, if you'll just work with me, you'll be able to see what I can't." David snorted at his word choice, but Sam went right on. "You'll come at this from your logical, intense, black-and-white view of the world, and you'll put the pieces together."

David swiveled his chair, listening to the creak of leather and the doubts in his head. He wanted to pray, to ask for guidance, but he was afraid. Afraid God wouldn't hear him. Even more afraid the answer would be no. He swallowed, clenching and unclenching his hands.

"Well, Dave? How about it?"

"I don't know how much help I'll be, but I'll give it a go."

Sam pounced on the box, as if he wanted to get started before David changed his mind. "Let me read to you a list

of things that have gone on at the mine over the last ten
months or so. Where'd I put my notebook?"

"Is this it, sir?"

"Thanks, Buckford." Pages scraped and shuffled. "Here it
is. Any one of these alone wouldn't draw too much attention,
but when you list them, it becomes more than a coincidence."

Sam read and David tried to organize the items into a
mental list, visualizing them in his head the way Rex had
taught him:

1. *Axle broken on new wagon. Team put down. Reason for
   failure unknown.*
2. *Ordering mistake leaves company store short on inventory.*
3. *Store robbed and ransacked. Four teams of mules stolen.*
4. *Shipment of faulty blasting caps. Work halted for two days
   till replacements are found.*
5. *Pumps falter. Time lost repairing and replacing parts.
   Reason for failure unknown.*
6. *Square sets fail, mine collapses. Eight dead, five wounded.
   Reason for failure unknown.*
7. *Transport bucket winch system fails, bucket falls to bottom
   of mine. One man injured, leg amputated. Winch and
   motor in good repair. Reason for failure unknown.*
8. *Pump fails entirely in No. 3 shaft, shaft flooded. Reason
   for failure unknown.*
9. *Ghost story begins to circulate. Men restless. Some walk off
   the job and hire on at competing mines.*
10. *Stope output in No. 3 well below predictions. New tunnel
    produces nothing.*
11. *Office ransacked.*

David's brows came down. "What? Predictions showed
shaft three should have the richest ore."

"We were delayed having to clear the debris from the

cave-in. Then the shaft flooded when the pump failed, so we had to install another pump. When we could finally send in the crews, we found nothing but rock. Then the standby pump failed. No sense throwing hard effort down a wet hole with no silver in it." Sam resumed his chair beside David. "None of us wanted to quit on it, not with all we'd lost trying to bring it in, but in the end we just had to abandon the shaft. Marcus urged us to keep trying, said we were losing faith with you if we stopped, but with no results. Father finally called a halt to digging in that tunnel."

Heat tracked across David's chest and up his neck. How could he have been so wrong? All the indications had pointed to a rich vein and stable rock to dig through. "I was so sure." He took a deep breath, then set his abacus flat on the desk. "I want to go over every page. Start with the earliest ones you've got, and we'll work our way forward."

Sam riffled the papers. "Buckford, can you sort through this box and put it all in chronological order? I'll start reading these. Dave, you stop me when you need to."

Sam read slowly, and David sat very still, absorbing, visualizing the charts and reports in his old handwriting, remembering and immersing himself in the work he had loved so much. He asked Sam to repeat some things and asked for clarification and expansion on others. Several times he did calculations on his abacus, but mostly he listened and collated the information to get an overall understanding of the data at hand. "You didn't read the initial survey and sample sheet I did on shaft three. I need to hear that."

"I don't have those. Not ones you did, at any rate. I have the ones Marcus did."

"No, I need the ones I did last June. My name should be at the top of every page. When I told Father I suspected there might be a rich vein there, he told me to handle all the preliminary work myself and not to bring anyone else in on it. There should've been no reason for Marcus to have filled out survey or sample sheets."

"I'll look again." Sam shuffled papers, rolled and unrolled charts, and shifted chunks of rock around. "I can't find any survey for shaft three other than this one Marcus did."

David shook his head. "Read out Marcus's report then." As Sam read, David tried not to give in to the growing doubts. "Those don't match at all."

"The question is why not?"

"You sound like you have an idea."

"You won't like it, but. . .think about it, Dave. Besides you and me, who has had access to everywhere in the mine *and* the store *and* the offices? Whose name is on this report? Who would know enough about mining to make sabotage look like random accidents?"

David shook his head, not wanting to believe it, though the doubts had been growing with every new report. "No, I can't believe that. Marcus? That's impossible. Our own cousin? He wouldn't do such a thing, not after all we've done for him."

Buckford spoke up. "That's quite an accusation. If you voice it outside this house, you will have to substantiate it. A very serious business."

Sam rapped his knuckles on the desk. "Men have died. Whoever did this is responsible not only for the loss of revenue and the loss of equipment, but also for the lives of eight men, plus the wounded, including David."

"But, Marcus?" David asked again. "Why? Why would he do such a thing?"

"I don't know. I don't know what his motive could be. The only hard evidence we have is this report. We know the figures here don't match what you originally surveyed. We know you found a rich strike in shaft three, but according to this"—the paper popped, and David envisioned Sam holding it up and jabbing it with his finger—"shaft three is a played-out dead end. And we can expect that if Marcus is the guilty party, then when he finds out I'm here in Denver talking to you, he's going to be on his guard."

David put his elbows on the desk and his forehead on his fists. "If it turns out that Marcus is behind this, Father is going to be devastated. We can't do anything more here. The answers we need are in Martin City." They would have to go. He would have to return to the scene of his accident. Clammy sweat broke out on his skin. He would never enter a mine again. He couldn't. Too many nightmares, too many shattered hopes, too many dangers, physical and mental, lurked in mines.

Sam put his hand on David's shoulder. "The minute we show up at the mine, Marcus will have to be suspicious. I would be. When we get there, we won't have much time. He'll either run or he'll try to destroy whatever evidence remains that could tie him to the sabotage." His hand dropped away. "Buckford, throw some things in a bag. We can leave on the morning train."

David slipped his watch from his pocket and touched the hands. "It's late. If we're leaving early, we'll need to get to bed."

Buckford cleared his throat. "Excuse me, sir, but Mrs. Mackenzie is due to arrive this week."

David jerked. He'd been so absorbed in the discussion and so focused on the task he'd completely forgotten Karen's return.

"David, just what's going on with you and Karen?" Sam put the question to him gently.

David rubbed his palm down his face and turned toward Buckford. "Sam and I will take the morning train. You'll stay here and await Karen's arrival. After the situation with Marcus is settled, I'll come back here and hear what she has to say."

"Very good, sir." Though Buckford would never contradict his employer, David got the feeling Buckford thought the plan of action anything but "very good."

When David and Sam were alone, Sam asked, "What's going on with you and Karen? Why didn't you go with her to her aunt's funeral? I hate to think of her dealing with all of that by herself."

David shook his head. "She preferred to go alone, so I gave her the space and distance she wanted." He gave a brief outline of events leading up to her departure, not sparing himself in the telling. "When she gets back, she might very well ask for an annulment." The idea lanced his heart, and he chastised himself. He had no one to blame but himself. She'd tried every way she knew to love him, and he'd pushed her away. He'd brought about the very thing he feared. She no longer loved him, and he'd lost her for good.

Sam sighed. "I'd like to lock you both in a room until you straighten things out. You've been going about this all wrong. Instead of giving her space, you should've held her and kissed her and groveled. She was looking for comfort and strength from you. At the very least, you should've written and told her how much you missed her and how you needed her and wanted her to come home."

"Since when did you become an expert on women?"

"I never claimed to be an expert, but even a blind man can see that a wife needs her husband to want her in his life. And eventually, everyone has a breaking point. You've pushed and tested and tried Karen to the limit, and she broke. It's up to you whether you want to attempt to put the pieces back together."

"What if I can't? What if it's too late?"

"What do you have to lose by trying?"

sixteen

With every mile of prairie she passed, Karen tried not to hope David would meet her train but failed miserably. Checking her watch didn't make the time go faster, but she couldn't stop. She had so much to tell David, so much forgiveness she needed from him. In the back of her mind, a niggling doubt taunted her. What if David couldn't forgive her? What if they really couldn't find happiness together?

Passengers sidled down the aisle, their canes, umbrellas, and valises jostling and vying for space. Though she wanted so badly to hurry them up, Karen forced herself to sit still until the majority of the occupants cleared the car.

She scanned the faces through the window searching for David's. Weak morning sunshine trickled through thin, high clouds, promising warmth.

Karen made her way outside. Baggage carts lined up beside the train. She picked her way over three sets of tracks to the platform and joined the stream of people heading up the stairs to street level. As she emerged into the terminal waiting room, she caught sight of Buckford standing by the ticket windows.

He waved and nodded to her, then crossed the tile, weaving around people to get to her side. "Welcome home."

His familiar face gladdened her heart, but she couldn't stop herself from looking behind him for David. "Thank you, Buckford." She adjusted her coat collar and checked her hat, trying not to be disappointed. There were so many people and so much noise and confusion she didn't blame David for not coming. "I can't wait to get to the house. Tell me, how is David?" The question uppermost in her mind came tumbling out. "Is he anxious for me to get to the house?"

Buckford cleared his throat and took her valise. "I'm sorry, ma'am, but he's gone to Martin City. Sam came to Denver and enlisted his help with some trouble at the mine. They've gone up there to rectify the situation."

"He's gone?" Her heart lurched. "When?"

"They left yesterday morning. The situation at the mine is most urgent."

She reached out and grabbed the valise from Buckford and started toward the ticket windows.

"Ma'am, where are you going?"

"Martin City."

"I'm supposed to take you to the town house to wait for him to return."

Karen stopped and looked up at him. "I am tired, Buckford. I'm tired of being apart from David. We've been apart in one way or another since last fall. This is going to end now. You are welcome to come with me, but I'm going."

He took the valise once more, a resigned cast coming over his features. "Very well, ma'am. If you'd like to go to the ladies' waiting room, I will procure the tickets. The westbound train won't leave for an hour yet. There will be time to get some coffee and send word to Mrs. Webber at the house. Would you like me to telegraph ahead to Martin City to let them know we're coming?"

"No. I believe we'll just surprise them."

"Of that I have no doubt, ma'am."

Arriving that evening in Martin City brought Karen a feeling of having come full circle. Was it only five months ago she and David had left for Denver, he wounded and embittered, she uncertain and wary? They had both changed and grown in those months, but was it enough to move forward to have something better than they possessed right now?

She swallowed and twisted her fingers while Buckford

lifted her bags from the back of the surrey he'd rented at the livery. Lights shone through all the ground-floor rooms of the Mackenzie home, beckoning. Piles of dirty, slushy snow lay along the foundation and mingled with the smell of smoke and hot metal from the smelters, the damp promise of spring settled over her. She knocked on the door.

"Why, Karen! Buckford!" Matilda enveloped her in a hug, pressing her cheek to Karen's in a gesture so reminiscent of Aunt Hattie's that Karen had to blink back tears. "What a surprise. Come in, come in. Jesse will be thrilled to see you. David didn't mention you were coming. I thought you were still in Kansas City. Please, dear"—Matilda drew Karen along into the house—"do accept our condolences on your aunt's passing. I know you must miss her terribly. Buckford," she tossed over her shoulder, "it's so good to see you again. As well meaning as the new man is, he's not you. Leave the bags. I'm sure Mrs. Morgan will want to sit you down in the kitchen for some coffee and a good talk."

Before Karen could get a word into the conversation, she was seated in the parlor sans cloak and gloves and accepting a cup of hot, sweet-smelling tea.

"Now, I expect you're very anxious to see David, but I'm afraid he isn't here." Matilda picked up her knitting and settled into her chair.

"Isn't here?" Dismay trickled through Karen. "Buckford said he set out on yesterday's train."

Matilda laughed and touched her temple. "I didn't mean he isn't in Martin City. I meant he isn't in the house. I don't know what kind of miracle worker that tutor you hired is, but David is a changed man. So confident, so focused and sharp. He was almost like his old self. This morning they had hardly finished breakfast before they were off and out of the house. Sam said not to wait up for them, because they would most likely be gone late into the night."

Karen could hardly fathom her mother-in-law's descriptions. A confident David, like his old self? He ate breakfast with his family, and he'd left the house voluntarily? Had being separated from her been that beneficial to him? Her sense of loss grew. How was she to reconcile with a man who thrived without her?

Matilda went on. "I'm so glad to know you've met the new pastor who's coming later this summer. Pastor Hamilton? You'll have to tell me all about him. I was so sad when Pastor Van Dyke said he was retiring, but I suppose it comes to all of us in time. Though I don't know that Jesse can retire. I think he'd dry up and blow away if he had to stop working."

Karen put her cup down and asked the question foremost on her mind. "Matilda, do you know why David came back home? I wrote him when my train would arrive, and when I got to Denver, he was gone."

The knitting needles stopped clicking, and Matilda's brows formed straight lines over her eyes. "None of the Mackenzie men would tell me anything. When Sam and David arrived last night, they took Jesse into the study and closed the doors. Whatever it is must be serious. David wouldn't have come otherwise, not with you expected back."

Karen wasn't sure about that. Her return to Colorado might have been the thing that sparked his flight to Martin City. "And you have no idea what it might be about?"

"No, just that it was mine business. It is good to have David involved again. I know you must've been disappointed that he wasn't there to meet your train, but it has to feel good to know he's here and working again." Matilda smiled. "I know you only went along with the lawsuit idea to please me and because we were out of options at that point, but you have to admit, it's all turned out beautifully."

❧

The next morning, Karen paced the flagstones of the conservatory behind the house. She should start gathering the flowers Matilda had sent her to get, but her thoughts tumbled and roiled like a snow-freshened creek in the spring.

David and Sam had not returned last night. Jesse came in near midnight, grave lines etching his face and his hair seemingly whiter than she remembered. He shrugged out of his coat, sagged into a chair, and put his face in his hands. "I don't know if the boys will be home tonight. They've been up at the mine office all day, and they're still working." He dragged his fingertips down his cheeks. "Matilda, I can hardly believe it, but Marcus is guilty. He's been systematically sabotaging the mine. They've tied him to nearly every disaster we've had over the last year. My own nephew."

Karen's jaw dropped. "Marcus? But why?"

Matilda rose and went to her husband, squeezing his shoulder and touching his hair. Jesse sighed. "We don't know yet. Nobody's been able to find him."

"Was he responsible for the cave-in?" Karen's mouth went dry. Marcus was David's cousin. His friend and coworker. Marcus Quint had asked several times for permission to come courting, though by that time she'd met David and wanted no other.

"They're still working on that one. They know he's guilty but not how he did it. The sheriff has a warrant for Marcus's arrest, and they're looking for him now. He wasn't on the night train to Denver. Beyond that, we don't know where he's gotten to."

As of this morning, there was no further news. Jesse had gone to the Mackenzie Mine to insist Sam and David come home for some rest. David should be here any time now. He'd be exhausted and in no shape for a discussion of his marriage. With everything going on with Marcus and the mine, it might be some time before they could talk things out.

She stopped pacing and picked up the clippers on the potting bench. She'd take some of the irises and some of the forsythia branches for a table arrangement. Calming herself, she breathed deeply of the warm, peaty smell of the hothouse.

Though Jesse teasingly grumbled about the cost of heating the greenhouse all winter, Matilda loved her flowers and Jesse loved her. He paid the bills and enjoyed the pleasure his wife took in the plants.

Gathering her armful of blossoms, Karen replaced the clippers and latched the door securely behind her. She could only see the chimneys of the Mackenzie house over the tops of the trees on the slope above her. Wending her way up the zigzagging path, she tried to avoid the dirty scarves of snow melting along the path. This early in April, further snowstorms were almost a certainty in Martin City, but for now a definite tang of spring flavored the air. She put her head down and hurried to get back to the house before the chilly air damaged the flowers.

Her heart jerked when someone stepped out of the trees onto the path, blocking her way. She had an instant to realize it was Marcus before he grabbed her and slapped a cloth over her mouth. Though she screamed, the cloth muffled the sound. Cold, hard fear throttled her senses. The flowers fell from her hands as she grappled with him, struggling for breath. Sickeningly sweet fumes invaded her lungs and blackness crept into the edges of her vision. Weakness suffused her limbs and everything disappeared.

❧

David awoke to a rock drill battering inside his skull. Stones jabbed his cheek, and when he tried to move, he thought his head might explode. Fizzing sparks snapped in his brain, but none stayed lit for long.

Footsteps scraped nearby and earth scritched as if something were being dragged across it. The sound echoed, and he became aware of. . .panting? The unmistakable smell of being underground enveloped him—dank, musty, earthy. "Who's there?"

A thump and quick rustle. "You should've stayed out cold."

Dread shot through David. "Marcus." His dry throat made his voice sound like paper crumpling. He coughed and wished he hadn't. "What are you doing?"

"This is your fault. If you'd have just stayed in Denver, everything would've been fine. You two made me do this."

"Two of us? Is Sam here? Sam? Where are you? Are you hurt?"

"Sam's not here, though I wish he was. His snooping brought you back here. If he'd have left well enough alone, I wouldn't have had to get rid of you."

Something soft subsided onto the floor. Satin brushed David's cheek and wisps of long hair feathered across his face. He tried to brace his hands against the ground to rise, but he couldn't seem to get his limbs to cooperate. A familiar perfume drifted to him.

Karen!

He tried to pull his thoughts together. How did she get here? Where *was* here?

"Why kidnap Karen? She has nothing to do with the mine. I still can't believe you'd do any of this to us. Why, Marcus?" He tried to keep Marcus talking, to stall the moment when he'd kill them both.

Marcus snorted. "Do you have any idea what it's like to always come in second place to the Mackenzies? Just because your name is Mackenzie, you think you're so much better than I." His voice echoed off the rock. "You should've been working for me. I had seniority. I had the experience."

Hard hands shoved David, and his cheek impacted a rock wall. Pain spun like a pinwheel in his head, making Marcus's voice sound far away. He gathered himself, gasping, trying to control the vertigo washing over him. "But we were kind to you. Took you in. My father paid for your schooling. Marcus, you're family."

"Your father crammed his charity down my throat until I choked on it. He was ashamed of me, of my parents—his own sister. He couldn't even bear to speak her name!" A clanking sound, like glass on stone. "Another dose with the last of this chloroform should ensure she stays out for a while longer."

A cloying aroma assailed David. "Stop it! Leave her alone!"

"Shut up."

An explosion of glass hit the wall over David's head and rained down on his hair and shoulders. His nostrils stung and his head whirled. David groped for Karen, his heart in his throat. The venom in Marcus's words made him sound on the verge of madness.

Her breath fanned his temple, and his heart started again. She was still alive.

Something clanked and squeaked. David, groggy from the knock on the head and the anesthesia permeating the air, inched his hand from beneath himself and felt around. His knuckles grazed wood then a metal wheel. A cart? He'd seen a hundred of them before, flat, with a metal pole on one corner to hang a lantern. Used to haul equipment from one tunnel to another. An icy finger traced up his spine. That must've been how Marcus got them underground by himself.

"Marcus." David clutched the edge of the cart. "What are you going to do? Don't leave us down here."

"Someone has to pay for what your family has done to me. Once I've blown the entrance to this mine, nobody will ever find you."

"Don't you think I've paid enough? I'm blind, Marcus."

"You've always been blind. You, the favored one. The one Jesse always bragged on. Your whole family is blind. There I was, right under their noses, and they never saw me."

A violent tremor started in David's core and radiated outward. He sucked in a staggering breath. "I can understand your anger at me, but why Karen? She has nothing to do with this."

"She has everything to do with this. Do you think you were the only one who loved her? She wouldn't even look at me after she met you. You took everything from me. I offered her all I had, but it wasn't good enough. She wanted you." He spat the words like vinegar. "You've no one to blame but yourselves. I want your last thoughts to be of how you wronged me." He grabbed David's shirtfront and shoved once more, cracking David's head against the wall.

Stars burst behind David's eyeballs, and a groan shot from his lips. He slid to the ground, gasping, trying to hold on to consciousness. Marcus's footsteps and the creak of the cart faded away, and David was helpless to stop him.

Time passed, though he had no way of knowing how much. He drifted in a murky half consciousness. Clammy sweat trickled down his temple and into a cut on his cheek, but the stinging was mild in comparison to the evil pain in his head and his inability to make it recede through sheer force of will. Far away a muffled blast sounded and a faint tremor rippled through the floor on which he lay. He finally gave in to the fog enveloping him.

seventeen

Hearing returned first. His own breathing and heartbeat. He became aware of time having passed and of being able to marshal his thoughts again, a little at a time.

Karen.

Had Marcus hit her on the head, too? He inched forward until his fingers brushed her dress. Satin, with velvet trim. The one she had told him was pale green.

He started with her head, touching her, searching for wounds, swelling, bruises. She made no sound, nor did she move again. He turned her from her side to her back, arranging her arms at a more comfortable angle, then felt along her ribs and down her legs. No blood or broken bones that he could find. He gathered her to himself, sliding back until he rested against the rock wall. Her hands were icy so he chafed them. Her head lay on his shoulder, and she fit perfectly in his arms. Gently, he kissed her brow.

When Father had come to drag him and Sam home this morning, he'd informed David that Karen had arrived. Sam had gone to the sheriff's office, and David had been waiting for him to return so they could go home. He'd assumed it was Sam's boots on the porch that he'd heard, but it must've been Marcus coming to get his revenge. Revenge that meant he and Karen were in the bottom of a mine shaft, shut in by an avalanche of rock and debris.

What if she didn't wake up? What if he'd lost her before he could tell her how much he loved her and needed her? What if he had to go through life alone?

His conscience kicked him and long-ago memorized

scripture filtered through his head.

> *"Whither shall I go from thy spirit? or whither shall I flee from thy presence? If I ascend up into heaven, thou art there: if I make my bed in hell, behold, thou art there. If I take the wings of the morning, and dwell in the uttermost parts of the sea; even there shall thy hand lead me, and thy right hand shall hold me. If I say, Surely the darkness shall cover me; even the night shall be light about me. Yea, the darkness hideth not from thee; but the night shineth as the day: the darkness and the light are both alike to thee."*

He wasn't alone. He was never truly alone. Though he had spend the past several months trying to push God away, considering himself unloved and unlovable because he had nothing to bring to any relationship, God hadn't abandoned him. Now that David had nothing left, he knew he had to turn back to God, acknowledge his sin and his need, and ask for forgiveness. He must make things right with God if he ever hoped to make things right with Karen.

David swallowed and flexed his rusty prayer muscles. "Father, I know I've been doing everything in my power to blame You for my blindness, for ruining my plans, or for just not caring. And all along I've known that wasn't true. I thought I was strong. Strong in body. Strong in mind. Strong in my faith. And in one blow, all that disappeared. But You've been there every step of the way. Watching over me, waiting for me to realize that I can't run away from You. Since the night of the recitations at the blind school, Your Spirit has gently reminded me of the truth."

His voice, though a whisper, seemed loud. Nothing he had done or felt or thought had escaped God's notice. Not his blindness, not his treatment of Karen, not his own pride in his engineering, and not his tantrums when his world blew apart and he couldn't put it together again. Remorse coursed through him.

"God, I'm so sorry. I've been such a fool, trying to blame You and fix everything on my own. I've made a colossal mess of things. I need Your forgiveness, and I need Your strength to show us a way out of here. I've so much to make up to Karen. I pray it isn't too late for us. I want to spend every day for the rest of my life proving to Karen I can be a good husband. Help me kill my pride over needing help."

He continued to pray as he waited for Karen to awaken.

❧

Karen fought her way upward through clouds of fog, forcing her mind to push through layers of cotton batting. A dull ache pressed against the backs of her eyes. She opened her eyelids a crack. Or at least she thought she did.

Nothing.

She lifted her sluggish hand up to make sure her eyes were open. They were.

But where had the light gone? Where was she?

Her breath came faster as she struggled to see even the tiniest spark of light. Before she could stop it, a scream rose in her throat.

Someone clamped a hand over her mouth.

She flailed, fighting to break free of the iron-hard arms that imprisoned her.

"Karen! Stop it! Karen, it's me, David!"

She stilled, her muscles stiff.

His hand eased away, and she tried to suck in a breath, but it snagged somewhere in the top of her lungs. She tried again, blinking and turning her head. She raised her hand in front of her nose but couldn't bring an image into focus. "David, help me! I. . .I. . .I can't see!" Her voice echoed, and she scrabbled against his shirtfront, seeking an anchor in the blackness. "I can't see." This time her words came out a whispered plea.

He clasped her to his chest, forcing her head onto his shoulder and stroking her hair. "Shhh. I've got you." He rubbed his chin against her hair. "You're not blind. We're in a mine. There's no light down here. He must've taken the lantern with him."

Karen clung to him, trying to make sense of his words. She squeezed her eyes shut then opened them wide, straining every muscle for the faintest glimmer of an outline, a form, anything in the dark. Her heart thundered in her ears. The blackness was a malignant thing, pressing against her. Her only point of reference was the security of her husband's arms. A mine? Why?

Memory came roaring back. "David, it was Marcus! He found me walking back from the greenhouse. He grabbed me." She grimaced. "He pressed a wadded cloth over my face, and there was a strange odor. I tried not to breathe it, but I must have. I don't remember anything after that." She pushed herself upright. "Did he do the same to you?" If only she could see his face. If only she could see anything.

"I'm afraid Marcus chose a more violent method to render me unconscious. He bashed me in the head."

"Are you hurt?" Her fingers flew, touching him, trying to find signs of injury.

His hands captured hers. "I'm fine, dearest. A little headache and some sore ribs, but nothing terrible." He pressed his lips to her fingers. "Are you hurt anywhere?" He brushed a kiss on her temple, and she pushed against his chest.

"How hard did Marcus hit you?" Her fingers moved upward, feeling the strong line of his jaw and the swelling and dried blood on his temple.

"Are you thinking I've lost my senses, darling?"

A lump formed in her throat. How she wished she could see his face, to judge for herself.

A chuckle—a chuckle!—leaked from him.

"You don't seem entirely yourself." What would she do if he truly was addlepated?

He hugged her close, rubbing his chin across the top of her head. "I certainly hope not. Karen, there's so much I need to say to you, so much to apologize for, but there isn't time. Suffice it to say, Marcus bashing me on the brainpan has finally brought me to my senses." He took her face between his palms and kissed her forehead. "I've made my peace with God, and the instant we're out of this mine shaft, I intend to begin to make amends to you. I've been a complete and utter fool where you are concerned, and I only hope you can find it in your heart to forgive me and start over. Oh, Karen, we have so much to talk through, but for now, we need to see about trying to get out of here."

Her breath hitched and the hollow, fluttery feeling behind her breastbone grew. "Do you think we can find our way out? Even in all this blackness?"

"The darkness won't matter to me. And remember, it doesn't matter to God. He sees us, He knows right where we are, and He can help us get out of here."

He brushed a kiss across her hair, and she wanted to weep at the miraculous change in him.

"Ready?"

"I think so, but which way?"

"Marcus's footsteps faded out to our right. If we go that way, we can be reasonably sure we're at least heading topside and not farther into the mine." He helped her to her feet. "I'll need both my hands free, but we don't want to get separated. Keep hold of my belt, and keep one hand on the side of the tunnel. If you stay right behind me, I can warn you about any low-hanging rocks or crossbeams."

Karen stumbled. "I can't seem to maintain my balance. I've never been in such utter darkness."

"That's how I felt at first, too, right after the accident.

Maintaining your balance does get easier after a while. Brace your feet wide apart and put one hand on the wall. Now, grab my belt, and we'll walk a few paces."

ঝ

David kept one hand above and in front of his head, and with the other, he maintained contact with the wall. The last thing he needed was to bash his already aching noggin on a crossbeam. Their footsteps echoed off the solid rock all around them, distorting distances and filling their ears. Every twenty or so paces, he stopped to listen, but only the sounds of their own breathing filled his ears.

David vaguely recalled the tremor and impact of what had to be Marcus blowing the entrance to the mine, but surely that would've drawn some attention. The family had to know he and Karen were missing by now, and they would be out searching. If David could find the mouth of the mine, would it be choked with rock and debris too thick for them to dig out? Perhaps the mine had more than one entrance or ventilation shafts. He knew he was grasping at thin straws, but what choice did they have? If they waited for rescue, they would die. If they wandered this rocky maze until exhaustion overtook them, they would die.

God, help us. You know where we are, and You know how to get us out of here. Guide our steps and lead us. Prayer was the only thing that kept despair at bay.

"How are you doing?" David stopped once more and reached behind him for her hand. She'd not uttered a single complaint as they inched along.

She gripped his hand and moved until his arm encircled her. Her head burrowed into his neck. "How far do you think we've come?" Her voice sounded small and weary.

"I wish I knew." They had to go so slowly, for fear of stepping off into space and plummeting down a vertical shaft. If only the mine would've had a narrow-gauge track, they could've followed it easily. He racked his brain for any clue as to where Marcus might've dumped them, but the slopes around Martin City were riddled and honeycombed with burned-out mining holes, and most had been plundered for any equipment and gear to aid in the next quest for treasure. He gave her what he hoped was a reassuring squeeze, then directed her hand to his belt in the back and started off again.

Karen stumbled. "Whatever Marcus drugged me with seems to be lingering. I can't think clearly."

"It might be the darkness." He talked to keep her spirits up. "Right after the accident I had a terrible time just organizing my thoughts. You'll be fine once we get you out into the light." He injected his voice with confidence, though his mind cringed at the reality of their situation. He couldn't tell if they were still heading the same way Marcus had gone. If they missed one side tunnel, they could wander down here until they dropped.

A faint, low rumble tickled his ears. He halted, straining to fix the origin of the sound, his heart in his throat as memories of the cave-in bombarded him. The tremor, the groan of rock, the cascading boulders and splintering wood—he stopped his stampeding thoughts and concentrated on the sound.

Water.

They edged along until the low rumble became a louder roar, the unmistakable sound of water falling into a pool. David turned and put his hands on Karen's shoulders. "Wait here. Sit down and don't move. I'll be right back."

"Can't I go with you?" She latched on to his hand.

"I'll only go a few paces. I need to check things out. I don't want to risk your tumbling into an underground river. Wait here and don't move." He squeezed her fingers and brought them to his lips. "I'll be right back, Karen. I promise."

Feeling with a probing toe and keeping one hand on the roughhewn rock wall, he crept toward the sound of the rushing water. The overhead lowered, and he had to hunch down, holding his bent arm over his forehead. Spray misted his skin, and the sound of the rushing water filled the rock-crevice and ricocheted. His foot swung over nothing, and he stopped and knelt.

Easing onto his stomach, he stretched his arm over the edge. The icy current caught his hand, dragging it from left to right. He could put his arm in up past the elbow, yet he couldn't touch the bottom. It was impossible to judge how deep it was. Sitting up, he grabbed a handful of pebbles and one by one he threw them in an arc around himself. Stone pinged on stone each time and plopped into the water. He retraced his steps.

"Karen," he called to her before he reached her. "Karen."

"I'm here." Her hands scrabbled for him, grasping on to his sleeve as if to a lifeline.

He put his arms around her. "We can't go that way. There's an underground waterfall and stream. I threw some rocks to see if the tunnel continued on the other side of the water, and there's nothing there but solid rock. I couldn't feel the bottom of the stream with my arm. The miners must've quit this tunnel when they hit the stream. We can drink here, but we'll have to go back and see where we missed a side tunnel. This is a dead end."

"A dead end." She spoke woodenly, as if her lips were stiff.

"Come on, Karen. We'll look on it as a blessing. We needed water, and we found it." He took her hand. "The overhead is low, so watch your head. And drink plenty. It might be a while before the next water."

❧

The jagged rock wall scraped Karen's fingertips, and her back ached. She tried to wet her lips, but her mouth was so dry. How long had it been since the stream? How many tunnels branched off this one? Were they in the main tunnel, or were they once again nearing another dead end?

When the third tunnel they'd tried ended in a solid rock wall, she wanted to sag to the ground and admit defeat. "Can we stop for a while?" She hated to ask. Stopping meant delaying their escape, but her legs wobbled and she knew she needed to rest.

"Are you all right?"

"Yes, just tired. I'm sure if I rest for a minute, I'll be fine."

"Come here." He took her elbow and eased to the floor, scooting until his back rested against the wall. He eased her down between his outstretched legs and pulled her back against his chest. His arms came around her shoulders and crossed under her chin.

Warmth and comfort enveloped her, and she leaned her head back. "How far do you think we've come?" Sleep tugged at her eyes, tired from straining to see in the darkness. She closed them, relaxing, her limbs growing leaden.

"I wish I knew. I wish I knew how far we had to go." He yawned and apologized.

"I'm sleepy, too. It feels like the middle of the night. What time do you think it is?"

"I had the same feeling, of it being night I mean. When I tried to check the hands on my watch, they hadn't moved, so I think it's broken. I must've landed on it when Marcus dumped me on the floor. If our senses are telling us it's night, it probably is." He yawned again, this time not bothering with an apology. "Rest, Karen. You'll need your strength. I'll wake you in an hour or so."

eighteen

"We need to get moving again, Karen."

Reluctant to wake, she snuggled closer into his embrace and wrapped her arms about his waist.

"Karen?" He stroked her cheek. "Wake up."

She eased upright, still caught in the gossamer wisps of a delightful dream—a dream where sunlight shattered in rainbows over everything in brilliant, vivid colors. David laughed and teased as he walked beside her under a never-ending sky, his hands in his pockets and his hat pushed back at a jaunty angle.

Then she opened her eyes. Total darkness. Persistent damp and grit. A cold wind blew through her chest, and the blackness pressed around her like an inky shroud. She knelt, hunching her shoulders and wrapping her arms at her waist with her head bowed. Reality obliterated the last shreds of her dream.

David groaned. "I got stiff sitting there so long." His hand grasped her elbow.

She gripped his arm to help her rise. "Ow!" Staggering, she hit the rock wall with her shoulder.

"Karen, are you all right?"

She pushed herself up, her lips tight against the pain. "Pins and needles." A million tiny stabs trickled through her legs. When the pain lessened, she took a few wincing steps. "There. That's better."

"Are you ready to keep going?"

She closed her eyes and gave her head a little shake. Panic fluttered through her chest and parched her mouth. "I can't remember which way we were heading before we stopped." If they chose wrong, they'd wind up right back where Marcus left them.

"Don't worry. Before we fell asleep, I slipped my watch out and put it on the ground. I laid out the chain in the direction we're supposed to head."

She sniffed back a few hot tears and swallowed the scream. "I never would have thought of that. You're so capable."

His hand trailed down her arm until he found her fingers. Lacing their hands, he squeezed. "You can't possibly know how much that means to me. I haven't felt capable for a very long time. Just knowing you need me gives me courage."

Grasping his belt once more, she braced herself to go on. If he could be courageous, after all he'd been through, she would be, too. They hadn't gone far when the hand she dragged along the rock wall brushed something metal. "Wait."

David stopped. "What is it?"

Karen swiped gingerly until she made contact with the metal once more. Thin, cold, driven into the rock. The jutting end coiled upward. "Just another candle holder." But no candle. Couldn't the miners have left *one* behind? When they got out of here, she planned to light every lamp and candle she owned, just for the joy of seeing them glow.

They continued on. Since turning back from the waterfall so long ago, David had suggested they walk almost side by side so he could keep one hand on one wall and she could keep one hand on the opposite wall, thereby hoping not to miss further branches that might prove to be the way out. But each tunnel they tried dead-ended.

David talked, and Karen was sure it was to encourage her. She tried to respond, but weariness, thirst, and an ever-increasing sense of despair made it difficult. How long since they'd had any water? She forced her mind back to what David was saying.

"I'm beginning to think we must be in the old Wildcat Mine. I could be wrong, but there are so many tunnels, branches, and offshoots. I can't think of another mine within a day's ride of

Martin City with such a labyrinthine layout."

"Will that help us, knowing which mine it is?"

"If I knew for sure it was the Wildcat, and if I could remember the details of the plan I saw one time, and if I knew exactly where in the mine we were. . ." He chuckled. "No, I guess it doesn't make any differ—" An odd *thunk* stopped him, and he plummeted to his knees, tearing her grip from his waistband.

"David?" Karen went down beside him. His hands pressed against his head, and he moaned. "What happened?" Her fingers flew over his face, taking in the tense jaw and the rigid muscles in his neck.

Through gritted teeth, he whispered, "Got distracted and hit my head on something."

"Is there anything I can do?"

"Just wait."

She scooted around to pillow his head on her lap and gently stroked his shoulder and upper arm. Eventually he began to relax.

"Does it hurt very much now?"

He sat up, and his arm came around her shoulders. "It's better. What a stupid thing to do, getting distracted and walking into a brace. I might have knocked myself out completely, and then where would you have been? Dead stupid."

"You're not stupid. You're the most brilliant, caring, wonderful man I've ever met."

David sat silent for a minute. Then he said, his voice rueful, "I'm surprised you would say that, Karen. Brilliance, caring, and wonder have all been sadly lacking in my treatment of you."

The soft caress in his voice broke her heart. "David, I. . .I. . ."

"I love you, Karen," he whispered against her cheek. "I know I haven't acted like it, but I've never stopped loving you." His hands came up to frame her face, and he brought his mouth down to hers.

With a grateful heart, she accepted his kiss.

Breaking apart, he rested his forehead against hers.

"David, I don't want to accuse you, but I need to know. . . why? Why did you put us through so much agony over the past few months?"

"I'm so sorry, my love. You can't know how I regret it. After Marcus left us here, I had a long time to think while I waited for you to wake up. I finally had to acknowledge the reasons behind my actions."

Karen held very still, not wanting to distract him from the words she needed to hear and the words she knew he needed to say.

≈

David breathed a quick prayer that God would slay his pride and help him conquer his fears, and he gathered his wife close. "The morning of the cave-in, I sent Sam and Marcus to the surface to go over some new figures. I was standing at the edge of the square-set framework I'd designed. Several miners worked the stope above and to my right removing ore we'd blasted a couple days before. A row of candles in their little holders flickered along the tunnel, each tiny flame giving enough light for the miner to see to dig. Paddy Doolin came toward me, pointing to the floor and yelling. I couldn't hear what he said over the sound of the drills and sledgehammers, but as he came closer, a shower of dust and pebbles fell from somewhere overhead. Then the framework groaned and cracked, and I knew it was all coming down. I think I yelled to Paddy to run, but it was too late."

His arms tightened around her, and his heart beat thick in his ears, reliving those moments when he thought he'd died. "I thought of you in that instant, Karen. While the rocks tumbled down around me, while the dust choked me, filling my eyes and nose and lungs, I thought of you and how sorry I was to be leaving you."

She stroked his upper back, clinging to him. When he could relax, she asked, "Then what happened?"

"I remember being trapped, pinned to the floor by rock and timber up to my waist. At first I thought I might suffocate, the dust was so thick. I managed to pull the collar of my coat up over my head as best I could and tried to breathe the air in that little tent. Rubble kept raining down on me. One good-sized rock or piece of timber must've come loose overhead and crashed into my temple. I blacked out."

Karen gripped his hand as if to give him strength and sympathy all at once.

"I don't remember Sam pulling me out. Father said Sam wouldn't leave the mine until he found me. I didn't wake up for two days." He swallowed and rubbed his thumbs on the backs of her hands. "When I did, I wished I had died in the mine. Karen, there's something in our family, something we don't talk about. In fact, once things were settled, Father forbade us to ever mention it. Most of it happened when I was just a boy, but the aftereffects have lingered on. So much so that you were caught up in them without knowing."

"What happened?"

"I told you once about my father's younger sister, Bernice?"

"Only that you said she was Marcus's mother and never to mention her because it was a sore spot with your father."

"That's right. Bernice was beautiful and vivacious and smart, and she married a man named Frank Quint. This was when we still lived in Ohio. When the Union called for soldiers, Frank went off to war, and when he arrived home a year later, he'd lost both his legs and his right eye. His face had been badly burned, and he couldn't do much for himself. Marcus was about fifteen at the time, and I was around twelve. I remember being horrified at the sight of Frank's injuries. Every time I looked at him, a shiver would race up my back. I wanted to help him, but I was repulsed."

He swallowed and laced his fingers through hers, pressing his palm to hers. "Bernice took one look at him and was sick. She refused to be near him, and at the first opportunity she left. His condition so disgusted her that she ran out on him. Father went after her and tried to drag her back, but she wouldn't come. Said she wouldn't be tied to a freak for the rest of her life, and that Frank would've been better off dead."

"What happened to her?"

"For a while she kept in contact with Marcus. She would send him letters from time to time all about her glamorous life. She spent some time on the riverboats, then went to New Orleans. Then one day a trunk arrived along with a letter. The steamer held all her belongings, and the letter was from a doctor in a sanitarium. She'd died of consumption after working in a brothel for a few years."

"That's terrible. What happened to your uncle Frank?"

"He went mad when she left him. Started drinking and talking to himself. He refused to bathe or eat, and he started hurting himself on purpose. Father tried to help him and was in the process of getting him committed to a hospital when Frank snapped. He drank a whole bottle of laudanum. He just couldn't face life without her."

"That poor man." Tears thickened her voice, and when he touched her cheek, his finger came away damp.

"I always wondered how he got the laudanum. Mother kept it locked in a cabinet in the kitchen. I guess a part of me always wondered if Marcus had given it to him." He took a deep breath. "So when I woke up unable to see, I guess I thought history was repeating itself. There I was, engaged to the most beautiful woman in town, and I was a cripple, like Frank. I did you a grave injustice fearing you would be like Bernice, but I was so afraid. I'd lost my sight, and at the time, I was sure I had killed several good men through my negligence. I hated myself and thought you would, too. Even if you didn't loathe me right away, eventually you would. Then you would leave me."

"So you tried to leave me first."

"I didn't want to be tossed aside as damaged goods." He stroked her hair. "Then my mother devised that entire lawsuit scheme, and I found myself married. I've never been more scared in my life."

She hiccupped on a sob. "I shouldn't have done it, but I was so desperate. Then you wouldn't take me as your wife, and I wondered if I'd made a terrible mistake. You threw the word *annulment* in my face."

"What I said to you on our wedding night was unforgivable, and yet, I do beg your forgiveness. It took everything I had in me not to open that door when I heard you crying, and yet, fear held me back. I thought you would be repulsed or I would be inept as a husband, and that fear kept me from you that night. And I feared fathering a child. Someone who would despise me like Marcus did his father. Someone who would be ashamed of his crippled dad."

She ducked her chin, and her breath came quickly. "I wish you would've told me."

"As I said, it was something our family was in the habit of not talking about."

They were quiet for a while. Then she stirred in his arms. "David, I'm so sorry for the way I acted when Aunt Hattie died. I shouldn't have blamed you."

"Ah, Karen, you shame me with your apology. I was the one who refused to go visit her. I was so wrapped up in my hurt and pride, afraid of being a burden to you, afraid of being the object of curiosity or worse, pity, that I kept you from being able to see her one last time. Then you went away and took my heart with you. I was afraid you wouldn't come back, or that if you did, you'd announce you wanted an annulment."

"I was so hurt and grieved I barely knew what I was doing.

I just knew I couldn't fight you anymore. I needed to get away to think, but I always knew I would come back. I'll admit your letter scared me, telling me to take all the time I needed. I thought you didn't need me at all."

He groaned. "I was trying to be supportive. If you only knew how I labored over that letter. I just wanted to ease your mind that Buckford and Mrs. Webber were taking care of me. You were the one who kept writing about how wonderful Pastor Hamilton was and about the matchmaking ladies of his church. You even mentioned that your aunt's lawyer was working on some annulment proceedings." He gave her a little shake.

"Oh, David, we've been rather foolish, haven't we? Is it too late to start over?"

His hand found her chin and lifted her face to his. Gently at first, but with the growing hunger of knowing they were at last free to love each other without misunderstandings, fear, or guilt, he took her lips with his own.

When he broke the kiss, she wiped at his cheeks, wet from her tears, and brushed her lips across his chin. "When you kiss me, when you hold me, I don't think of you as being blind. I just know I love you."

"As much as I'd love to stay here kissing you, I think we'd better get moving. But trust me, when we do escape this infernal mine, you're going to get a thousand more kisses, and you're never going to have to wonder if I love you."

She laughed and scrambled to her feet. "Is your head still paining you?"

Bracing himself against the wall, he pushed himself upright. "I'm a bit light-headed, but that might be relief and your kisses more than any crack on the skull."

"Then lead on. I want to get out of here and make you fulfill some of the promises you've just made to me."

nineteen

Rocks and ruts filled the floor of the shaft. Their progress had been slowed to a crawl by the jagged terrain. A dogged certainty that they were going the wrong way clung to Karen, making her sluggish.

"Careful, darling. There's a big rock to step over." David put his arm around her waist to help her over.

"The way is getting so rough."

"If things don't improve soon, we'll have to go back and try the other tunnel." He sighed, stopping for a moment. "I can't think that Marcus brought us this way. The going is too uneven for the cart he had with him." He started moving again, and Karen had to follow.

When the walls narrowed and the tunnel ended in yet another unyielding rock wall, Karen sank to the ground and let sobs overtake her. "I can't go on anymore."

David knelt at her side, lifting her to her feet, gripping her shoulders. "You can. You have to. Karen, you're the bravest woman I know. You won't let this defeat you. We *have* to believe we will get out of here. Don't give up now. You're brave, remember?"

"I don't feel brave, David. I feel tired and scared and small and lost. This darkness is pressing in on me. There's nothing here but rocks and timbers and blackness."

"I know how you feel, darling. I do. But you mustn't give in to the fear. Remember what it did to me? I let it paralyze me, but I refuse to be afraid any longer, and I refuse to let you be afraid. We're together. We have each other, and God hasn't abandoned us."

Karen licked her dry, cracked lips. "I thought I knew what you were going through with the blindness, but I didn't. I didn't know how horrifying it could be not to be able to see. I'm so sorry, David."

He laid his cheek against her hair, his hand rubbing her shoulder. "Shhh. None of that. We'll get through this together, right? There has to be an end to this tangled burrow, and we'll find it if we just keep going. We'll meet each obstacle as it comes, and if we have to dig our way out, we'll do that. By now, I imagine Sam and Father are moving mountains to get to us, literally. So we are not going to abandon hope, right?"

"Yes, David."

"I love you, Karen. Don't forget that."

They retraced their steps, and Karen tried to be brave, to pray, to think of anything that might get her mind off the despair that threatened to overwhelm her. Thoughts echoed and ricocheted in her head. She shook it to clear her mind. *Think! What's nagging at you? It's something David said.* "David?"

"Yes?"

"You said that just before the cave-in Paddy Doolin was coming toward you."

"Yes." They stumbled along a few more paces, and when she didn't continue, he asked, "Why?"

"Paddy Doolin's widow came to see us in Denver, right? I've been trying to think why he thought it so important for his wife to tell you about the wild animals. He must've been going to tell you just before the accident. You said he was coming toward you, pointing to the floor."

"That's right," David said, the doubt clear in his voice as he inched forward, keeping a tight grip on her hand.

"So what was under him? And what did it have to do with coyotes?"

"The floor was under him." He inched along a little faster, as if trying to escape her questions. "A few million tons of rock were under him. If he went far enough, China was under him."

"I'm sorry, David. I won't pester you anymore."

He stopped. "No, darling, I'm the one who is sorry. It's just so hard to think about. I feel so guilty. I should've been able to forestall the cave-in. I should've cottoned on sooner to what Marcus was up to, and for the life of me, I can't understand how he did it. It might very well have been a design flaw of mine that caused the failure." He stumbled, his grasp tearing away from hers as he fell.

"David!"

"I'm all right. The wall disappeared. I think I found another side tunnel."

She edged forward as his boots scraped on the rock. Groping for him in the blackness, she found the wall first.

He muttered and stretched away from her, reaching for something. "What on earth?"

"What is it, David?" Fear rose in her throat. If only she could see.

"It's a tunnel of sorts, but the opening is small. The base of this side tunnel must be three or four feet above the floor of the tunnel we are standing in."

"Why would they do that? Is it a ventilation shaft?"

"No, it's—" He stopped.

"What?"

"It's a thieves' tunnel." The wonder of discovery filled his voice and sent chills up her arms.

"What?"

"Why didn't I think of this? Of course. All the pieces fit." He gripped her shoulders. "Paddy Doolin was right! When he said coyotes, he didn't mean the ones he shot for raiding the henhouse."

"David, tell me what you mean."

"When word gets out of a possibly rich lode at a mine, there are always men who want to get to it before you do. That's why we keep things quiet when we think we're getting close to a big strike, right?"

"Right."

"We were very close to what I had a hunch might be the biggest strike we'd ever hit. My early boring samples indicated an extremely rich stope, more silver and lead per ton than we've ever pulled in before. And the only ones who knew about it were Father, Sam, me—and Marcus. It's possible that Marcus told someone or was working with someone to get to the stope first. When thieves want to get to the treasure, they don't file a claim, they don't start operating high, wide, and handsome. They dig narrow, tight, quick tunnels, looking to get to the strike first and take what they can before anyone is the wiser. Sometimes this is referred to as a coyote. Paddy Doolin must've seen signs of coyote digging and been coming to warn me. And if he was pointing to the floor, they must've been digging beneath the shaft." He gave her a little shake. "Don't you see it? The shaft didn't collapse from above. It collapsed from below."

"Then that means. . ."

"That means the cave-in *was* sabotage. I *didn't* do anything wrong." Relief radiated from his words. "Karen, I think this coyote tunnel may be the answer to our prayers." He sucked in a harsh breath. "I didn't want to tell you, because I hoped it wasn't true, but before he left us, Marcus said he was going to blow up the entrance to the mine. I've been praying for another way out, just in case, and here it is."

Blow up the entrance to the mine. She pressed her hand to her middle, as if she could stay the feeling of her insides turning to sand and trickling away. "You mean. . ." She swallowed, praying her knees would hold her up. "I'm glad you didn't tell me before now. I'm not sure what I would've done."

"I know it won't be pleasant, since it is so cramped, but this tunnel should lead us to the surface. Are you willing to try?"

"How cramped?"

"It will be big enough for us to get through, but not tall enough for us to stand up straight. And it might angle up pretty sharply, depending on how deep we are, but it probably doesn't have any offshoot tunnels. Thieves don't waste time. It's dig straight for the treasure and get out quick."

"If you think it is best, then, yes, let's go."

"I'll go first to make sure it's clear." He climbed into the hole, sending a cascade of pebbles bouncing to the floor. His hands reached back for her. "Here, I'll help you up. We'll have to crouch and go carefully. If I say stop, you stop right away."

After eons of climbing in the narrow shaft, her knees hurt and her palms burned from contact with the rough rocks. A hundred knives pierced her hunched back. "Can we rest for a minute?" Ever since David had realized he wasn't responsible for the deaths of his friends and employees, he'd been rejuvenated, picking up their pace, hopeful of reaching the surface soon. Karen had been so happy for him and so thankful for a way of escape from the mine, she had done her best to keep pace, but the long hours in the dark had taken their toll. She couldn't go on without a break.

David must've sensed her despair. "Yes, let's rest. Come, let me hold you for a minute."

She sidled near him and eased down. Feeling his arm, she reached for his hand, content to sit side by side with her head on his shoulder for a while.

He yawned and drew his knees up as far as the cramped shaft would let him. "Strange as it seems, and as long as we get out mostly unscathed, I can't say I'm sorry for this experience."

She choked on a breath. "You're not?"

"I know. It's odd. But would we have been as open with each other? We had so many misunderstandings and things to hash out. I thought you were leaving me for good; you thought I wanted you out of my life. When you left, I was still fighting with God about being blind, and I was afraid to leave the house. Our marriage was dying under the weight of my pride. If God hadn't stripped me of everything and allowed Marcus to kidnap us, I don't know when I would've broken down and asked for forgiveness. I was pretty useless to myself and everyone around me."

"How could you think that? My life is nothing without you."

"Do you know how long it has been since I thought you really needed me? Do you know what it's been like to have you be the one to arrange our transportation, hail cabs, see to the mail, pay the bills? I know you're more than capable, but I wanted to be the one to do those things for you. I was used to being in charge."

She tried to imagine what it had been like for him, and her fingers curled around his. "David, I need you for so much more than you can even imagine. I've never felt put upon taking care of mundane tasks like paying bills. I do those things because I love you, not because I'm trying to take control. You're the head of our home."

He kissed her temple. "Are you rested enough? Think you can go on?"

twenty

"Did you feel that?" David stopped, and Karen bumped into his back.

"What?"

"I thought I felt...fresh air?" He sniffed.

Karen pushed her hair off her face and tried to swallow. The universe consisted of nothing beyond plodding in the dark, the scrape of their shoes on the rocks, and the persistent ache in every muscle and joint. The dank, dusty, earthy smell of the mine had clogged her nostrils for such a long time, she didn't know if she would recognize fresh air.

"There, there it is again." David's voice lifted. "We're almost there." His hand reached back for her and took her hand to help her along once more. "Can you see daylight?"

She forced her eyes open wider and strained to focus on anything. Disappointment washed over her. "No, I'm sorry. I don't see anything."

"Maybe we're around a bend." They stumbled on.

Gradually, Karen became aware that the darkness wasn't as black. Her heart lifted. "David, I see—"

"What? Sunlight?"

"No, I think it's...starlight?"

"That makes sense. We must've been walking all night. Can you see the opening?"

"Not yet."

With each step, objects and shapes began to emerge from the gloom. She discerned David's outline, hunched shoulders, torn shirt, and tattered pants. Dried blood and dirt caked his hands in dark streaks as he sought handholds to help them up the slope. "David, I can see it. About ten yards ahead maybe? I can see stars through branches."

"Do you want to go first, since you can see it?" He stopped and spoke over his shoulder.

Tears pricked her eyes and altered her voice. "No, David. You've led us this far. You go first." A cool breeze that smelled of night dew brushed her cheeks.

David reached the opening and swiped his hand across the bramble stretching across it. Twigs snapped, and the opening widened. "We made it." David shouldered his way through the limbs of tiny new spring leaves, and once free, turned back and held out his hand. "We made it, Karen."

She struggled the last few steps up the rocky slope and all but fell into his arms. Tears wet her cheeks, and she clung to him. "Thank You, Lord. Thank You, Lord." Her light-starved eyes took in every contour of the hills, every tree and shrubby shape. Pale stars winked overhead in an indigo sky. Fresh, sweet, cold air swept over them and murmured in the sparse pines, and somewhere a cricket chirped.

"Can you tell where we are?" David lifted his face to the wind and breathed deeply.

Karen loosened her grip on him and turned to survey the valley below and the hill behind them. "We're about halfway up a fairly steep hill, and there's a creek in the ravine below. You can just hear the water."

"That's our first priority, then. I don't know about you, but I could use a drink of water about now."

They skidded and slid down the slope. Loose stones and tufts of grass made the going difficult, but eventually they reached the water. David moved with more confidence than she would've thought possible just a few months ago, keeping hold of her hand until they knelt beside the creek.

Water had never tasted so good. She cupped her hands again and again, wetting her neck and splashing the front of her dress in her haste. When she couldn't hold another drop, she sighed. "Which way do we head now?" Weariness crept over her again, and her limbs turned to lead. If only she could curl up and take a nap. She chafed her hands, icy after plunging them into the stream.

"Downstream."

She didn't question him. "The creek curves to the left around this hill."

"I know you're tired, but the sooner we get back to town, the quicker someone can get after Marcus."

Rocks littered the streambed and made for slow going. Tailing piles from played-out mines lay like giant tongues on the hillside. They picked their way around the base of the hill, and Karen kept a watch out for a lamp or sign of habitation.

She found none until they rounded the brow of the hill, and she stopped to get her bearings. Above them, she thought she caught the glow of firelight. The skeletal frame of an abandoned derrick lay twisted, hanging down the slope as if pushed over by a giant's hand. A sharp, new scar marred the earth, darker than the surrounding dirt and rocks. "David, there are people up there. Can you hear them?"

"Where?" His face turned to the sound of rocks and men's voices.

She hugged him. "We're rescued. I think there's a road here. . .or at least a path. It zigzags up the grade."

Halfway up, the muffled noises clarified into the sounds of digging and men shouting. A mule brayed, and metal implements struck rock again and again.

"Hello?" David shouted, but the work above didn't stop. He tried again. "Hello!"

"What can they be doing in the middle of the night?" Karen stubbed her toe on something. Her skirt caught and she had to stop and free it. "David, you said you thought you knew which mine we might've been in. What was it called?"

"The Wildcat?"

Karen lifted the board she'd stepped on and angled it to get a better look. "I think you were right. I've got a piece of a sign here. It says Wildcat Mining."

The sound of timber splintering cracked through the air, and cheers went up. "We're making good progress now. You men with the pickaxes, get started on those boulders."

"That's Sam!" David's face brightened. "They must be digging for us."

With the last of her energy, Karen climbed the hill. David kept his hand on her shoulder, and at last they topped out on a little plateau. Bonfires roared in a semicircle around a pile of boulders and shattered wood. A dozen men crawled over the rocks, lifting them down and carting them away. Dust sifted through the air and swirled in the breeze.

"Sam!"

She sank to the ground, exhausted. Sam broke from a group of men and charged toward them, grabbing David by the arm then pulling him into a hug.

"You're alive! How did you get here? We've been digging for hours."

Karen could barely see through her tears as David tried, between backslaps and handshakes, to explain how they got out of the mine. Someone pressed a warm cup into her hands and dropped a blanket around her shoulders.

Sam knelt before her. "Are you all right? We've been worried to death."

She sipped the coffee, letting the hot liquid warm her from the inside out. "I'm fine. We're both fine. Just so very tired."

"Right. Explanations can wait. Let's get you two home."

❧

Nothing had ever felt as good as the hot bath and clean nightclothes Matilda prepared for Karen. She fussed and mothered, supervising the bath and washing Karen's hair for her. All the while she marveled at their escape and at the changes in David. "David seems so much like his old self. I don't know what happened down there, but I'm thanking God for it."

Karen eased her feet into the lamb's wool slippers Matilda had warming by the fire and stuck her arms into the sleeves of a thick wrapper. "I am, too. We got off to a rocky start, but everything is wonderful now."

"Praise the Lord." Tears glistened in Matilda's eyes, and she turned away, swiping at her cheeks. "Now, drink this tea. Then it's bed for you."

The clock struck six times. "No, there's something I want to see first." She padded downstairs to the study, following the sound of male voices. She stopped in the doorway, still holding her tea.

David, freshly tubbed and in a dressing gown, stood by the fire, leaning his forearm against the mantel.

Sam sat on the corner of the desk, one booted leg swinging. Dust and dirt streaked his face and clothes, and sweat plastered his hair to his head. "Marcus had a snitch in the sheriff's office. The minute we left there after getting the warrant, one of the deputies ducked out and ran right to Marcus."

"How did you know we were in the Wildcat?"

"When Karen didn't come back from the greenhouse, Mother got worried and went down there. She found flowers all over the path and sent Buckford for us. We were climbing the walls because you were missing."

Jesse rocked in the chair behind the desk. "I knew in my gut that he'd come for you both, but we had no idea where he would take you or what he'd do to you."

Sam turned his hat in his hands. "Then a couple of men came belting into town yelling that there had been an explosion on Wildcat Hill. Father remembered that Marcus had done some work for Wildcat Mining just after he finished his schooling."

Turning his back to the flames, David tucked his hands into the pockets of his robe. "Where's Marcus now?"

Sam swallowed and darted a look at Jesse. Jesse's brows lowered and the lines beside his mouth deepened. "Marcus must've misjudged the explosives. We found him in the rubble. He's dead, David."

Karen's hands shook, sloshing her tea.

Matilda appeared at her shoulder and took it before it spilled. "Come away, Karen," she whispered. "You need your rest."

Karen shook her head.

David shoved away from the mantel. The blood had drained from his face. "Do you think it was an accident, or did he take his own life, like his father did?"

Jesse flinched. "He was under a lot of pressure. We don't know what was going on in his head. Accident or not, it cost him his life."

Sam stood. "You girls can quit hovering in the hall. We're done talking. I'm going to get cleaned up. Mother, don't you think Karen should be in bed?"

Karen inched into the room and stood on tiptoe to place a kiss on Jesse's cheek first then Sam's. "I won't be long out of bed."

Jesse hugged her as if she were spun glass. "Drag David upstairs with you. He looks terrible."

The family filed out, leaving David and Karen alone.

"It's not true, you know." She crossed the room and wrapped her arms around his waist, leaning her head against his chest. He smelled of soap and clean linen. She breathed deeply, her eyelids heavy.

"What's not true?"

"You don't look terrible. You've never looked better to me."

His heart thudded steadily under her ear.

"I'm sorry about Marcus."

He nodded. "Why aren't you in bed? You're practically falling asleep in my arms."

"I can't think of a better place." She smiled. "I wanted to wait for you, and I knew if I got into bed, I'd fall asleep before you got there."

They walked out of the study arm in arm and up the stairs.

At the landing, she stopped. "David, the sun is up." Faint warmth came with the light, and she squinted against the brilliance. "Can you feel it? The dawn of a brand-new day."

A Letter To Our Readers

Dear Reader:

In order that we might better contribute to your reading enjoyment, we would appreciate your taking a few minutes to respond to the following questions. We welcome your comments and read each form and letter we receive. When completed, please return to the following:

Fiction Editor
Heartsong Presents
PO Box 719
Uhrichsville, Ohio 44683

1. Did you enjoy reading *Before the Dawn* by Erica Vetsch?
   ❏ Very much! I would like to see more books by this author!
   ❏ Moderately. I would have enjoyed it more if

   _____

   _____

   _____

2. Are you a member of **Heartsong Presents**? ❏ Yes ❏ No
   If no, where did you purchase this book? _____

   _____

3. How would you rate, on a scale from 1 (poor) to 5 (superior), the cover design? _____

4. On a scale from 1 (poor) to 10 (superior), please rate the following elements.

   ____ Heroine   ____ Plot
   ____ Hero   ____ Inspirational theme
   ____ Setting   ____ Secondary characters

5. These characters were special because? _____

_____

_____

6. How has this book inspired your life? _____

_____

_____

7. What settings would you like to see covered in future
   Heartsong Presents books? _____

_____

_____

8. What are some inspirational themes you would like to see
   treated in future books? _____

_____

_____

9. Would you be interested in reading other **Heartsong
   Presents** titles? ❏ Yes ❏ No

10. Please check your age range:
   - ❏ Under 18   ❏ 18-24
   - ❏ 25-34   ❏ 35-45
   - ❏ 46-55   ❏ Over 55

Name _____

Occupation _____

Address _____

City, State, Zip _____

E-mail _____

RUGGED & RELENTLESS

Jacob Granger is chasing down his brother's murderer. His only clue?—a circled and most unusual ad that leads him to Hopesfall where he cashes in on his logging experience and pretends to court Evelyn Thompson. Will this feller find himself falling for the entrepreneurial female and foregoing his lust for vengeance?

Historical, paperback, 320 pages, 5.5" x 8.375"

Heartsong♥ng

HEARTSONG PRESENTS TITLES AVAILABLE NOW:

(If ordering from this page, please remember to include it with the order form.)

Presents

Great Inspirational Romance
at a Great Price!

Heartsong Presents books are inspirational romances in contemporary and historical settings, designed to give you an enjoyable, spirit-lifting reading experience. You can choose wonderfully written titles from some of today's best authors like Wanda E. Brunstetter, Mary Connealy, Susan Page Davis, Cathy Marie Hake, Joyce Livingston, and many others.

When ordering quantities less than six, above titles are $3.99 each.
Not all titles may be available at time of order.